The Lady's Home

The Brownville Series

Stevie Lynne

Stanhy L.L.C.

Copyright © 2025 by Stevie Lynne

All rights reserved. Published in the United States by Stephanie Funk dba Stanhy, LLC.

No part of this book may be reproduced in any form or by any electronic or mechanical means, including information storage and retrieval systems, without written permission from the author, except for the use of brief quotations in a book review.

No part of this book was created with artificial intelligence (AI).

Any resemblance to any persons living or dead, and any places is strictly coincidental. This book is a work of fiction.

ISBN: 978-1-7362150-3-6

Library of Congress Number: 002455257

It takes a village...
To my husband for believing with me, and my friends who have encouraged me to continue creating through thick and thin.
And to Block Island, where I escape to write and create in peace.

Chapter One

At 2:57 a.m. exactly, Betty started shrieking.

It wasn't the screams of passion they had all been enduring up until about 2:48 a.m. ...this was something else altogether.

Lily Harris, Doris Winslow and Rita Tiernan reached the confluence of the upstairs hallways outside of Betty's door at almost exactly the same moment. Rita, her hair in pink plastic rollers that hung askew, clutched her frayed flannel robe as she pounded on the door to Betty's room.

"Betty! Betty, what's wrong?"

A muffled shout punctuated by a sob reached them through the polished oak door. Lily looked frantically at Rita, her glasses hanging crookedly on her narrow face, frayed sweatpants and her dead husband's tee shirt, her night clothing of choice. "What did she say? Betty! Betty? What's wrong?"

There was a bleating cry from inside the room. "I can't breathe!"

"Oh, for heaven's sake!" this was from Doris, clad in a

long sweeping nightgown buttoned to her throat, her gray hair in tight precise curls even at this hour of the morning. "Get out of the way!" She shoved Rita aside and grabbed the knob.

It wouldn't budge.

"Damn it all! She locked it again. What did we tell her about locking herself in?"

Rita sniffed, "Well, I think the reason why is obvious. She's gone and brought herself home another man."

Lily rolled her eyes. "Well, DUH! Of course she did! Why do you think none of us have slept a wink tonight?"

"Well, you don't have to be snarky about it!"

"And you don't have to be simple about it either!"

"Ladies! Ladies! SHUT UP! Rita, where are the spare keys for the rooms?"

Rita looked vaguely down the wide hallway, the light reflecting off the polished wooden floor and the paneled walls. "Let me think..."

From inside the room came another pleading cry, "Get him off of me, please!"

"Oh, for heaven's sake." Doris reached up and grabbed one of the plastic pins holding Rita's curlers. "Get out of the way!" Creakily, she knelt down and inserted the pin into the lock.

"What are you doing?" this from Rita.

"What does it look like I'm doing? I'm picking the damn lock is what I'm doing!"

Rita reached up and caught her now dangling curler. "How in the world do you know how to do THAT?"

Doris looked up at her wryly. "You teach 6th grade for 42 years and see the skills YOU learn on the job. There..." The door swung open. "Betty? Betty, what's wrong?" Doris clambered to her feet unsteadily.

The room was silent.

Cautiously, the three women pushed the door open further and peered in. By the light cast from Betty's clock on her nightstand, they could see vague details of the room before them; the window with faint light seeping in around the curtain, the four-poster bed that contained a lump...a large lump. And an arm hanging limply off the bed from beneath the lump.

"Betty!" Doris headed into the room at a turbo waddle, the fastest her arthritic joints would allow, with Rita and Lily close behind.

Rita fumbled for the lamp on the nightstand, knocking something heavy onto the floor with a splat. She pulled the cord and light bloomed.

"Betty! What the heck?" Rita's jaw dropped.

Betty was lying on her back, her head tipped to her left shoulder and her jaw hanging slack. Her arm dangled limply off the bed. She was out cold.

And the reason she was out cold was sprawled on top of her in all 375 pounds of naked glory. His arm dangled next to Betty's and his head was tipped away from the women, showing them the distinct bald spot on the top of his head.

Unfortunately, the rest of him was very visible...and very naked...on top of Betty, whose face was starting to turn blue.

"Jesus! Get him off of her!" Doris grabbed a flabby upper arm and tugged fruitlessly. Rita gingerly grabbed his ankle and Lily went to grasp his paunchy buttocks.

Doris tugged grimly. "Come on! We have to get him off her now! Jesus! Why won't he wake up?" She shook his arm hard. "You! Get off of her!"

There was no response.

Betty gave a gurgle.

"Pull him off of her!" Doris shouted.

Lily reached over and slapped his butt cheek sharply, the sound snapping through the room. "Hey, you, wake up now!"

He remained inert.

"We don't have time for that! Rita, Lily, you two take his leg, the far one. I'll take his other arm. We can roll him off her and onto the floor. Go on! Grab it now, and on the count of three, we all pull him over toward us."

"But we're going to see his pee-pee!" Rita was aghast.

"Good Lord woman. If you've seen one, you've seen them all. Come on, let's do it before she dies!"

"Oh nooo..." Rita grasped the man's knee, turning her head away and closing her eyes. Lily grabbed his ankle. "Ready."

Doris leaned over him, grimacing in pain, and firmly grabbed his upper arm. "One...two...THREE!"

The lump on top of Betty slowly rolled up onto his right side, then bonelessly slithered off the bed, landing with a squishy crash on the floor. He lay inert.

"Betty!" Lily clambered over him onto the bed. "Betty!" She grabbed her shoulders and shook her.

Betty gasped and arched her back, drawing in a huge, raspy breath. "AhhhhhUhahhh!"

"Jesus, Betty, what did you do? Did you give him some of Rita's Ambien or something?"

"Hey! Leave my stuff alone!"

Betty gagged and gasped, croaking out a faint, "No. He made a weird noise and then he went limp. Gahhhhhh!" She dragged air into her lungs.

"Betty." Doris was kneeling beside the man on the floor, her fingers on his neck. Something in the tone of her voice made the other women look at her as Betty slowly hauled herself up into a sitting position. She, like the man on the floor, was naked, and she, like him, was not something they wanted to be seeing in the flesh. Her breasts hung limply below her navel. Once a 38D, she could now be called a 38 long.

Rita averted her eyes.

"Betty," Doris said again. This time she made eye contact with her. "He's dead."

"Oh damn..." Betty breathed.

There was a moment of silence. Doris looked sharply at the man's face for a moment.

"Where did you meet him?" her tone was urgent.

"I, uh, I went over the Legion Hall across the river. They were having a campaign fundraiser for someone. We met at the bar, and he was a fine specimen of a man, so I asked him if he wanted to come back here for a nightcap. Why? What's wrong?"

Doris stood up slowly. "Lily, hand me that quilt."

Lily dragged the pink and green quilt off the bed and handed it to her. Doris draped it haphazardly across the man. She looked hard at Betty. "Do you THINK you could give us all a break and cover up?"

Betty flushed, and pulled the twisted sheet over her torso, much to the relief of the others.

"Where are his clothes?"

"Huh? Why?"

"Just tell me where he put them."

Betty pointed across the end of her bed. "He left them in the bathroom."

The hem of Doris's nightgown hissed across the wide

plank floor as she rounded the end of the bed and disappeared into the bathroom.

There was a rustling sound then... "Oh hells bells!"

"What?"

"What?"

"What?"

The three women said in unison.

Doris appeared in the bathroom doorway; her face was paler than her gown. She held a driver's license in her hand.

"Betty. Who is this man?"

Betty's brow furrowed. "He...he told me his name was Ricky."

"Ricky what?"

"I...I dunno, I didn't ask. All he told me was it was Ricky and that he was up here for the day. I liked him!"

"Oh, sweet Jesus." Doris grimaced at the license in her hand. "Betty. This is Richard Haverill."

Lily and Rita gasped. Betty frowned, puzzled. "Who?"

Doris closed her eyes briefly. "Richard. Haverill."

"I guess that name is kind of familiar...but I can't say why."

Rita's eyes were round. "Betty! He's famous. He's running for Vice President."

"Vice President of what? The Legion?"

"NO!" Rita's voice broke into a squeak at the end. "Betty...he's running for Vice President of the UNITED STATES!"

Betty's mouth rounded into an 'o' and she stared at the pink and green covered lump.

"No."

"Oh yes," Doris said grimly, "And now he's as dead as a doornail on YOUR BEDROOM FLOOR!"

Tears sprang into Betty's eyes.

Lily scowled, "Oh come on now; you didn't even know his name!"

Betty looked up, her brown eyes swimming with tears. "You don't understand. He was my first celebrity screw...I didn't even know it...and now he's dead!"

Chapter Two

Rita gently placed the tea pot on the dining room table in front of the three silent women. She slid out the chair and joined them.

The room glowed softly from the massive chandelier above, a bizarrely gaudy touch after the morbid scene upstairs.

Lily carefully poured tea into the four china cups.

She set the pot back down. For a long moment, the only sounds were those of the nighttime; faint traffic noises from over toward Main Street, the gentle hissing of the wind in the tree branches outside.

"We have to call the police." Rita finally broke the silence.

Doris was shaking her head. "Do you have any idea of what a shit storm this will be? The man is running for Vice President of the United States. He's Horace Rock's right-hand man, the next in line for the Presidency if they win! Do you have ANY idea of how bad it will be if they find out he died here, in Betty's bed? They're going to think we killed him!"

Betty rocked back and forth, her arms wrapped around herself. "Well, technically I did. I mean, one minute we were having a hell of a go and then the next, BAM! And of course he had to go and die RIGHT before I was about to have an orgasm too. What is it with men? They always have to leave you hanging like that."

"BETTY!" Rita's jaw hung slack and Lily stifled a laugh.

"You gotta admit, she's right!" Lily snorted again, then began to laugh.

Doris drew herself upright and stared disapprovingly at her. "Lily Harris. You just pull yourself together right now! We have a problem here! A big one!"

"Oh, it's a big one alright. Did you see the size of him? He must weigh almost 400 pounds. Jesus Betty: couldn't you have found an insignificant little guy to haul home this time?" Lily fixed her with a stare.

Beside her, Rita clapped her hands over her mouth. Her shoulders shook and muffled giggles began to escape from around her fingers. Lily leaned forward and put her head on her arms on the tabletop. Her body began to quake as silent laughter rocked her. Betty stared for a moment then started to chuckle, that little "Heh heh heh," she had. Doris sat straight upright, her mouth quivering. She covered it. To everyone's astonishment, strangled chuckles erupted from her throat.

The four women burst into raucous laughter. Tears ran down Lily's cheeks. A snort like that of a rooting hog escaped from Doris, setting them off into paroxysms of laughter.

Slowly, the laughter slowed and stopped.

Betty wiped tears from her face. "I swear to God, I had no idea who he was."

"Betty, you never know who ANY of these men are! You can't keep doing this! You're almost 80 years old!" Doris had regained her indignation.

Betty sniffed, "Well, I certainly don't LOOK it."

That was true: and it was causing more issues than not in the past eight months.

"So, what are we going to do?" Lily asked into the lull.

Rita shook her finger firmly at them. "We HAVE to call the police!"

Doris was already shaking her head no. "If it was anyone else, then yes. But we CAN'T call the police for someone like Richard Haverill. Dear Lord...do you have any idea of the ramifications of that? No, we need a plan. We need to get him out of here and back to where he was. Let someone else find him. Betty, where was he staying?"

"Uh oh..." Betty had her hand over her mouth.

"What do you mean 'uh oh'?"

"He told me his bus was going to leave about an hour after we hit it off and all, so I told him I would drive him to the airport tomorrow. I thought he meant a public bus."

"Well, it would appear not. That 'bus' he mentioned is the campaign bus. Oh, holy hell. They've probably already missed him."

Doris drummed her fingers on the table.

Rita chimed in, "I can look up their schedule on the computer. Maybe we can drop him off at the next stop." She got up and shuffled out of the dining room.

Betty crushed her fist into her mouth. "I had no idea I was going to be causing so much trouble! I just thought he was a fine hunk of a man."

Lily rolled her eyes.

"Well, we can't call the police or life as we know it will never be the same here. These politicians are all the same;

they're always rooting around like a bunch of oversexed swine. Hopefully, they won't miss him right away, or if they do, they'll keep quiet about it instead of risking a scandal." Doris said.

Rita shuffled back into the dining room, her expression glum. "The New Hampshire stop was the last one on this tour. They are heading back to Washington, D.C. And I looked Richard up, too. His wife is on a cruise this week, and he was slated to have a few days off before a white tie fundraising dinner in the Capitol next weekend. He's supposed to be one of the guests of honor."

"Oh damn." Betty sighed.

Doris looked off into the distance, her eyes unfocused. "Rita, can you find out his office address in D.C.?"

"Sure, I guess."

"And look up his home address, too."

Doris stared at her cooling tea, slowly twirling the mug around.

"What are you going to do?" Lily asked.

Doris looked up, her eyes flinty. "WE are going to take that man back where he belongs."

"Back home?" Betty was aghast. "But D.C. is a full two-day drive for us, maybe longer! How are we going to get a dead man 'home'?"

"You do know he's going to start stinking soon, right?" Lily, once a dairy farmer's wife, was the pragmatic one.

"And how are we going to get him into his house once we get there?" Rita had reentered the room in time to hear the last part.

"We'll figure something out." Doris replied. "For now, we need to try to get his clothing on him before he gets all stiff.

"Ewwwww!" Betty responded.

Chapter Three

The women sat in silence for a moment. Having lived together for as long as they had, they were comfortable in quiet moments. The Lady's Home was the local name for the graceful old mansion they shared. Started some twenty-odd years ago as a retirement home for widowed and single elder ladies, the home had long been a comfortable, quiet retreat.

Doris grimaced as she considered the ramifications of the press finding out a leading contender for the Vice Presidency, a married contender to boot, had died in the embrace of a lustful, if slightly demented 79-year-old.

The prospect wasn't appealing.

Then there was the matter of Betty to consider. More and more, she had been acting erratically, forgetting things she shouldn't have. Of late, she had taken to bringing home men at every turn, some married, some not, some old, some not.

And when she wasn't hauling some stranger home, there was that damn incessant buzzing coming from her room at all hours of the day and night.

When this was over.... IF they got out of it okay...Doris was going to make damn sure she went over to see Doctor Parker for a full neurological workup. Something was clearly not right with the once mild mannered, quiet woman who had moved in 12 years ago.

Doris massaged her temples as she turned the problem around in her head. They were in Brownville, VT, a short hop across the Connecticut River from New Hampshire where this disaster had started. Brownville was a close-knit community, which was a double-edged sword for them. On the one hand, she could reach out for help when it was needed. On the other hand, it meant keeping a secret in this town was well-nigh impossible.

And then there was the problem of Betty. Doris regarded her thoughtfully across the dining room table. Betty had been stunning in her youth, and that beauty was still there, faded and a bit tattered, but there. Her hair was white but looked blonde, her cheekbones were high and her eyes a smoky amber color. Her body was still remarkably lithe.

With the right outfits, tastefully applied makeup and the soft lighting, she quite often passed for a woman 25 years her junior.

It wasn't until the clothing came off that the truth came out, but by then most men simply rolled with it.

Clearly, that had happened tonight.

The thing of it was it hadn't been an issue all these years. Oh, Betty had dated men and had brought them home over time, but they were boyfriends, long-term beaus.

This proclivity toward one-night stands was new. And frequent. And alarming. They had discussed it before now, with the vague resolution that they needed to have an intervention with her, and soon.

It hadn't happened yet.

And now it was too late.

Doris sighed and pushed her teacup away from her. "Ladies, we have to get him out of the house."

Rita put her hand to her mouth. "Where are we supposed to put him? And what will we do with him?"

"We will work that out. But first, he needs to get out of this house now. Before he gets stiff."

"And before he starts to stink." Lily added helpfully.

"Eww," Betty and Rita exclaimed in unison.

Doris slapped her hands on the polished table, her curls bobbing slightly on her head. "FOCUS! How are we getting him out of the house? He's not a small man!"

"Boy, I'll say." Betty replied dreamily.

Lily looked at her, aghast. "Do you think you could get your brain out of your panties for a hot minute and help us figure this out?"

"You're just jealous." Betty pouted.

Lily rolled her eyes.

"Lily," Doris said thoughtfully, "How did you and Bud deal with dead cattle when you had the farm?"

"Oh gross!" Rita cringed at the question.

"Well, we used the loader mostly. Tie up the legs with a chain and suspend them from the bucket. Then we could drive them over to the pit to bury them.

"Well, that's not going to help. We don't have heavy equipment here." Doris drummed her fingers in frustration.

"You know, sometimes they went down in places we couldn't get a loader into, and we had to get them out by hand." Lily stared into the distance, replaying moments in her mind. "When that happened, we had a homemade skid we used, something we could drag them out with.

"Yes! Yes. That would work. Tell me how you made it?" Doris leaned forward, her eyes on Lily.

"It wasn't anything fancy, just some heavy-duty plastic that Bud got when the old BemCo factory shut down. We cut handle holes on it and fastened ropes. You could slide it under the cow and once it was in place, a couple of people could drag her out of the barn to where we could use machinery."

"Oh." Doris sat back, disappointed. "We don't have anything like that."

"But we DO have all that plastic drop cloth the painters left last month." Rita sat up excitedly. "I watched an episode of 'True Crime in the City' where someone used that to move a corpse. They just rolled him up and he slid across the floor like a watermelon seed."

"Eewww!" Betty recoiled.

"You have any BETTER ideas, Betty?" Doris fixed her with her schoolteacher glare. Betty shrank down in her chair.

"N...no. I just don't like the thought of poor Ricky all wrapped up in that plastic!"

"Well, maybe 'poor Ricky' should have kept his pants on. He might still be alive had he done that."

Lily stood up. "The plastic is in the garden shed. I'll go get it."

Doris rose creakily. "I'm going to get dressed. Come on, girls, let's get him out of here before daybreak."

Betty asked, "What are we going to do with him?"

Doris shook her head. "I don't know. Let's get him out of here and into the car. We can figure it out from there."

Chapter Four

Doris cautiously pushed the door to Betty's room open. Rita, Lily and Betty crowded in behind her, peering over her shoulder.

"What if he's not dead after all?" Betty asked in a stage whisper.

"What do you man, 'if he's not dead'? He's dead. He's VERY dead!" Doris hissed.

"But I saw a documentary where people were thought to be dead, and they weren't. They just went into this coma or something."

Doris turned and stared at her incredulously. "And did their hearts stop too? Because that man over there has NO PULSE and NO HEARTBEAT. He is very, very dead."

"Well...I don't know, I mean what if..."

From the dim recesses of the room came a noise. The ladies jumped and gasped.

"Jeepers! What was THAT?" Lily yelped.

Rita started backing into the hallway. "This isn't funny. We need to call the police!"

"You know we can't do that." Doris snapped. "Quiet! What was that sound?"

The ladies strained to listen in the silence.

After a few moments, Lily said, "I guess we were just hearing things."

From the depth of the room came a rumbling fart.

"Gah!" Rita turned and sprinted away. Doris jumped backwards into Lily shrieking, "Oh my God! He's alive! He's alive!" Betty slapped her hands over her mouth. "Oh my God! Oh my God!"

Lily incomprehensibly started laughing. She shoved Doris away from her.

"No, sillies. He's dead. In fact, he is very dead. He's letting off gas. The cows used to do that too. My land they would fart after death. Made the boys on the farm jealous."

Rita peered around the corner of the hallway at them. "He...he's truly dead? And he can still fart?"

"Oh yes, they most certainly can."

Doris regained her composure. "Well, come on then. The sun's going to be up in an hour. We don't have a lot of time to waste!"

Betty looked dubiously down the hallway. "So, I can see getting him down the hall, but then what? How do we get him downstairs?"

"We could use the dumbwaiter!" Rita had rejoined them. "We could let him down right into the kitchen and get him into the car from the back door."

"I guess that could work." Doris said thoughtfully. "If it can handle his weight, that is."

"We better move fast before he starts to stink." Lily added helpfully.

"Will you stop saying that? God!" Rita huffed.

"Hey, I'm just telling you what's coming. We may have

an hour to daylight, but we may have less time before he is impossible to move. Once he gets stiff, it's gonna take hours for rigor to break."

"Oh gross." Rita screwed her face up. "That's disgusting."

"That's life. And death. Everything that lives dies."

"But did it have to die in Betty's bedroom?" Doris huffed. "Come on. Let's do this."

The four women tip-toed into the dark bedroom, giving the lump on the floor a wide berth.

Lily leaned over, fumbling for the pull cord on the bedside table lamp.

The lump on the floor gently farted again.

"Oh gross!" Lily took a step closer, then stumbled, falling into the bedside table. She caught herself on the edge as the lamp tipped sideways. She grabbed it just before it fell. Shoving it upright, she found the cord and tugged. "What is on the floor here? I just stepped on something round and hard."

Doris turned and looked at her feet as the light flared to life. "Wha...what in Sam Hill is THAT?"

Lily looked down as Rita crowded closer. Betty stared at them blankly from the other side of the quilt covered lump.

"Is that.... is that a...?" Doris stammered to a halt.

Lily started laughing again. "That most certainly IS what you think!" She turned to Betty, "How come you're bringing men home when you have a bull sized dildo on your floor?"

Betty brightened. "Oh! That's Frankie!"

"Frankie?" the three women repeated in unison.

"Yes. Frankie. Frankie keeps me happy on the nights I don't have a man with me."

"Is THAT the buzzing noise I've been hearing from

your room?" Rita's face was slack jawed with astonishment. "I thought you were brushing your teeth!"

"At 2:00 a.m.?" Lily asked her.

"Frankie helps me sleep. You know since I've gotten, well, a little bit older that it's a lot harder to sleep now. Frankie helps me with it."

They stared at the dildo in silent astonishment. "Is that supposed to mimic a human?" Lily asked. "Because I've seen horses who were smaller than that!"

The pink and green lump on the floor let loose with another rumbling fart.

"Come on, ladies. Never mind Frankie here. We have work to do." Doris turned to Rita. "Bring that plastic in."

"Are we going to put his clothes on? I really don't want to see that again." Rita was backing away, her lips quivering.

Lily rolled her eyes as Betty picked up the dildo, gently cradling it. "Will you put that thing away already? Jeeze Louise!"

With a sigh, Betty slid her drawer open and gently deposited it inside. "There. You happy now?"

"Gross." Rita muttered, "Just gross. It's bad enough you have that...that thing in here, but you had to go and name it too!"

"Well of course Frankie has a name!" Betty turned to her, her hands on her hips. "What am I supposed to yell when I start to have an..."

"STOP! Just STOP!" Doris shouted.

The women fell silent.

"Lily. Get the plastic in here. Rita, go get his clothing out of the bathroom. Betty, do you THINK you can help us get his damn clothes back on?"

Rita came out of the bathroom with the dead man's

clothes draped over her arm. She held a pair of shiny black shoes in her other hand.

"Come on." Doris said to her, "Let's get this done."

Lily rustled into the room, a double armload of plastic hissing across the floor. "Here. I brought all of it. You really think this will work?" she asked Doris, her brow furrowed.

Doris shrugged. "I have no idea, but we also have no option. Let's get him dressed and rolled up."

It was devilishly hard to dress a corpse. Lily muttered a curse as his arm flopped again, refusing to cooperate and slide down into the sleeve. Mercifully, he was still limp, but lividity was setting in with dark bruises forming on his side. He flopped bonelessly onto his back as Betty tugged gamely at his pants.

"I've done my fair share of UNDRESSING them, but I can honestly say this is the first one I've DRESSED." She sat back on her heels looking at her handiwork. His white button-down shirt was buttoned crookedly, the pants refused to fasten at the top. Doris knelt down creakily with his red necktie in her hand. Grimacing in distaste, she threaded it through and started knotting it.

Rita waited beside them with the dark suit coat in her hand. She looked at the American flag on the lapel.

"Betty, how could you not know this man was one of the politicians? I mean, look at how he is dressed. For heaven's sake, you had to be blind not to see it!"

"No blinder then he was to not be able to tell she was almost 80." Lily added.

"Hey!" Betty clambered to her feet; her hands fisted. "You two knock it off!"

"Ladies, LADIES! Focus!" Doris held warning hands up between them. "We are running out of time! The sun's going to be up soon."

On the floor the corpse gently farted again.

"Come on! We need to get Ricky the Gas Factory out of here!" Lily dragged the plastic over and started unrolling it as Betty and Rita worked at fitting a beefy arm into the suit coat.

With much grunting and groaning from the women (and a few more farts from the recently departed Ricky) they managed to finish dressing him and wiggled the plastic under and around him, rolling him up like an overweight burrito.

Panting slightly, they stopped to survey their handiwork.

"Think we can move him now?" Rita asked nervously.

"We sure as hell better hope so." Lily replied.

From inside the plastic wrapped burrito came another fart.

"Jesus!" Lily exclaimed. "Let's get him out of here!

Chapter Five

Gray light was starting to seep in around the curtains.

Doris straightened up and massaged her back. "Lily, Betty you two take the feet. Rita and I will take the head. On the count of three, we will lift him up."

"What are we going to do with him?" Betty asked.

"Get him down to the dumbwaiter like Rita suggested. Grab a corner everyone. One, two, THREE!"

The women heaved on the plastic.

The corpse stubbornly refused to lift.

"Come one, again. One, two THREE!"

Rita lost her grip on the slippery plastic, falling backwards against the bed before bouncing off and landing on the corpse.

"Ewww! Oh God! GROSS!" She scrambled up.

"Well, this clearly isn't going to work." said Lily. "How about we do it like we did with the cattle?"

"And how did that work?" Doris asked.

"We dragged 'em."

"Oh, ick!" Betty turned away, her hand to her mouth.

"A little late to be squeamish, don't ya think?" Lily asked.

Doris was gingerly bending over. "Come one then. Grab your corners. We will drag him down the hallway then."

With the four of them tugging, the slippery plastic bundle began to move. They tugged and jerked it across the room, then through the doorway into the hall.

They stopped and looked down the hall in dismay.

Betty's room stood at the junction of the two hallways, where most of the bedrooms were located, kind of an L shape at the end of the house. To get to the dumbwaiter they were going to have to drag him the length of the center hallway, then around the corner to where the old servant's quarters used to be. The dumbwaiter was midway down that hall on the right.

To get there they would be dragging him the length of the hall and past the main staircase to the foyer below.

It seemed an impossible distance.

"Come on, ladies. We don't really have a choice here."

"We can call the police and tell them what happened. We didn't do anything to him!" Rita wrung her hands.

"Yeah, except dress him again and wrap him in plastic. That's going to go over well with the Brownville, PD." Lily responded wryly.

"So, we unwrap him and leave him here."

"Rita, you know that's not an option. Come on now: he's not getting there on his own!" Doris slowly bent over and grasped a corner of the plastic again.

This time, thanks to the navy throw rug outside of Betty's room, the bundle began to slide easier. With much grunting and groaning, the women began to make the laborious trek down the hall, which was looking impossibly long.

They reached the top of the polished wooden staircase that swept gracefully down to the ground floor. Rita stopped with a groan. "I have to...I need a...gosh. I just need to take a break for a moment."

She dropped the corner of the bundle with a thunk. Betty let go of her corner, just as Doris shouted, "Rita! No! Not he...."

The slippery bundle was perched right at the top of the polished wooden stairs. When Rita and Betty let go of their ends, they were both on the same side, leaving Doris and Lily with the opposite side still in the air. The bundle teetered, farted again and started slithering down the staircase as gravity took over.

"Oh! Oh! No!" Doris shouted.

Lily dug in grimly, but the weight was too much for her. She let out a yelp as she lost her grip. With a sighing rustling noise, the late Ricky Haverill began to slide down the staircase, picking up speed as his mass took over.

"Oh!" the ladies cried in unison as the corpse slammed into the front door and halted in a crumbled heap.

They stood in stunned silence.

"Well, at least he's downstairs now." Lily said brightly.

Chapter Six

"This has turned into a total mess." Rita huffed.

"As if it wasn't already?" Doris replied. She heaved a shaky sigh. "Okay...okay. Time for Plan B."

"What's that?" asked Betty.

"I don't know, but we're going to find out." Doris began to gingerly make her way down the staircase.

Lily paused on the second step down, rubbing her chin speculatively. "You know, maybe this will work out okay after all."

Doris glanced back at her. "What do you mean?"

"Well, we have a bigger door to get it...I mean him... through. Then a short slide down the front steps. I bet we can pull the car right up next to the stairs, maybe even just huck him inside nice and slick."

Doris reached the foyer with Rita and Betty trailing behind her. They looked dubiously at the plastic wrapped bundle that Betty had been having sex with mere hours earlier.

"How in the world are we going to get him into the

car?" Rita asked. "I mean, we could barely get him off of Betty and all we had to do was roll him onto the floor."

The four were silent staring at Ricky as he gently farted inside the plastic wrap.

"Well, we better get him out of here right quick, because you know he's going to start to stink soon."

"Ew, Lily will you STOP saying that?" Betty balled her fists as her chin quivered. "He was my lover!"

Lily rolled her eyes.

Doris rounded on her sternly. "Enough of that! Both of you! We need solutions, not bickering. We need to get him out of the house and into the car at least. Then we can take a moment or two to think through our next steps." She rubbed her face with a shaking hand. "So how do we lift such a large...thing...into the car?"

Lily brightened, "I have an idea!"

"What? What is it?"

"If we can drag him out on the front porch, we can use the garden cart. Tip it toward the step and shove him feet first down them. He'll slide right into the cart sweet as pie that way."

"And then what?" Rita asked.

"Why we roll him over to the Buick and tip him into the back seat."

Doris looked dubious. "I don't know. The lawn is awful rough and uneven there. I don't think we can roll the cart from the front porch all the way over to the car." She looked down at the plastic bundle and frowned. "And this looks awful. It LOOKS like a corpse. What if someone goes by and sees us?"

"No one is going to see us, Doris. I swear, you worry too much."

"Well, SOMEONE has to! We are in a pickle here, a

pretty big one I might add!" Doris fixed a glare at Betty. "And I HOPE no one saw you two leaving the Legion Hall last night."

Betty pouted and pushed a lock of white hair back behind her ear. "It's not my fault he died you know. I guess he couldn't handle a hot woman!"

"Oh, for Christ's sake." Rita muttered.

"I'll go get the cart." Lily said.

"No, wait a minute first!" Doris held up a hand to stop her. "We can't take him outside looking like this. We have to wrap him in something else, something to at least cover the plastic up."

The women were silent for a moment looking at the bundle.

"Well, can't we just wrap that rug the rest of the way around him?" Rita asked.

"Yes! Yes, that's it! Betty, go in the kitchen and get that roll of masking tape out of the drawer. Lily and Rita, can you get that rug around him more? I'd do it but my hip..." she trailed off.

"Sure, sure we can." Lily said putting a hand on Doris's arm. "We've got this."

Lily and Rita tugged at the blue throw rug, working it up and around the body, covering the plastic. Betty came back with the roll of tape and wordlessly handed it to them. With much huffing, they laboriously worked the roll around the head, midsection and legs, taping him up like a large blue burrito.

At last, they rocked back on their heels and surveyed their handiwork.

"Now it looks like a corpse wrapped in a rug." Betty pointed out.

"Probably because it IS a corpse wrapped in a rug." Lily

said dryly. She stood up creakily. "We really need to get him outside and into the Buick. I'll go get the cart. Rita, can you manage bringing the car around? Pull it right up the lawn over here," she pointed through the sidelight window on the front door, "And get it as close to the edge of the porch as you can. Mind that rose bed though; those thorns will do a number on the paint."

Lily went in search of the garden cart and Rita hurried off to the kitchen to get the car keys.

Doris fixed a stern gaze on Betty who was staring blankly at the late Ricky Haverill on the floor.

"Betty. You cannot keep doing this you know. We've all been getting more upset about your...peccadillos of late. You keep us up half the night with these men. And now... this! How could you not know who he is?"

Betty's chin quivered as tears sprang to her eyes. "I'm just trying to have some fun while I can! I was only married to Brad for a few years before he died! I loved him, but we weren't like.... like THIS!" She waved her hand vaguely over the body.

"Like...what?"

"This, THIS! You know, like FUN. I loved Brad, don't get me wrong, but it was always 10 p.m. on a Sunday, Missionary style, and over in 10 minutes. It was not like THIS!" She waved her hand again.

"Oh, good Lord." Doris muttered.

Outside Lily clattered up to the staircase with the garden cart. The first red and gold rays of sunlight were touching the top of the old maple tree out front. Sycamore Street was still quiet, but that would change, and soon.

Rita carefully pulled down the driveway and began inching the car closer to the stairs, Lily guiding her. At last, they had the car positioned where they needed it.

Lily opened the rear door, revealing the Buick LeSabre's massive back seat. "We just roll him over and pop him in. There's plenty of room in the car. But he can't stay in it long. What are we going to do with him, dump him?"

Doris shook her head no. "I said we have to take him home."

"And how are we going to do that before he starts to decompose?"

"I don't know! We can get ice or something!" Doris's composure was starting to slip as exhaustion crept in. "Let's just get him into the darn car before someone sees us!"

Lily maneuvered the garden cart over to the steps and tipped it so the lip was under the second step. "Here. I'll hold the cart while you three slide him out here into it."

Rita looked dubious.

"Come on." Doris barked. "Ladies, let's do this before anyone comes by."

With much groaning, the women managed to slide Ricky back away from the door enough to open it.

Cautiously peering up and down the street, they propped open the massive front door, Ricky's corpse a blue clad mountain in the middle of the foyer. The three women grabbed the leading edge of the rug and began to pull. The lump quivered, then slide an inch, then two, then a foot.

Grunting, they hauled him feet first over the threshold onto the front porch. Mercifully, the floor of the porch on the 120-year-old house had a tilt like so many of the old houses did, a tilt that helped the bulk slide toward the stairs.

Sweat was running down their faces as they tugged and hauled the body toward the stairs. Lily nervously scanned the street, her head swiveling left and right.

They paused at the top of the staircase with the feet of the corpse sticking out into space. Rita staggered upright and leaned on the balustrade gasping for air. "I need a minute."

Doris leaned against a column, feeling her heart pounding out of her chest and her hip shrieking in agony. "Come on, we are almost there. Let's get him into the cart."

The women grabbed the rug again and pulled for all they were worth. Ricky slid an inch, then two, then more as gravity took hold. Lily held the cart up bracing for the impact. "Come on girls! We're almost there!"

With a herculean effort the women dragged the corpse off the edge of the stairs. It teetered for a moment then slithered down the stairs and thudded feet first into the garden cart. Lily yelped as the weight crashed down on her end of it. It tipped back down onto its feet with Lily dropping the handle and grabbing the bundle to stop it from sliding all the way out. It teetered and halted sitting up in the cart with the feet up on the handle and the upper body tipped forward.

"Yee haw! IT WORKED!" Lily shouted.

Doris was bent over gasping for air. She looked up at Lily and raised an eyebrow. "I...huff...thought...huff...you were certain...huff...it would work?"

Lily slapped her thigh triumphantly. "I HOPED it would work, but I was far from certain about it."

"Oh great!" moaned Rita.

"Well, the important thing is it DID work. Now all we have to do is get him in the car." said Betty.

The women fell silent looking at the garden cart.

"This...this looks a lot harder than you made it sound." Rita said finally.

"We can do it." Lily announced confidently. She went to raise the handle. The cart didn't budge. She tugged again. "Darn it all. Give me a hand here, you guys."

The three ladies came around and joined Lily, grabbing the handle. With much groaning they got the feet to lift off the ground and laboriously began inching the cart toward the car, which looked impossibly far away.

The sun was beginning to send thin fingers of light between the houses next door as they reached the yawning rear seat of the car. And stopped as they realized they would have to somehow drag the corpse up slightly to make it into the seat.

They dropped the handle of the garden cart and stood staring morosely at the car.

"Well, maybe we could..." Lily began just as they heard the rattling groan of an approaching motor.

They looked at each other wide eyed.

"What day is it?" Rita hissed.

"It's Monday." Betty said.

"Oh no.... that's Cyrus."

"Oh no, oh no, oh no!" Doris exclaimed. "NO! How could we forget today is when Cyrus comes?"

Lily wheeled toward the street just as the bright red panel truck with the lettering 'Morton's Dairy' on the sides rolled into sight, turning into their driveway just like he did every Monday.

But unlike every other Monday when he rolled to the back door to drop off two gallons of fresh milk and a carton of eggs from his hens, this time he slowed to a halt and stared at the scene in front of him, his brow furrowed over his bushy eyebrows.

Cyrus owned the only dairy left in Brownville, a dairy that still survived in part by him being able to establish a milk delivery route. He charged more than supermarkets, but his products were by far fresher and there was the satisfaction of supporting the local farmer instead of a grocery store.

At that moment, however, Doris fervently wished she was still supporting the grocery store instead.

He stopped the truck and leaned out the open door. "Morning Ladies. You need a hand with that?" He eyed the garden cart, baffled.

Lily recovered first. "Morning Cyrus. We're trying to take this old rug over to the Goodwill, and well, you know, it was harder than it looked."

"They'll pick up big stuff, you know." He shut the motor off and squinted. "And what are you doing out here at 6:30 in the morning, anyway?"

"I, ah, we uh, couldn't sleep last night so we decided to do something useful." Doris stepped into the breach. "We thought we could just do it ourselves."

"Well, I can give you gals a hand with that." He stepped out of the truck and adjusted his suspenders, red ones this morning fastened to blue jeans and over a green shirt with 'Morton's Dairy' over the left side of his chest and 'Cyrus' on the right. "Here, let me just get in there and I'll have it in the car in a jiffy."

Rita, Betty, Doris and Lily snuck horrified looks at each other as he leaned in over the corpse. Cyrus grasped the rug around the head and tugged. He stopped with a surprised look. "Why this darn thing is heavy! How'd you get it all the way out here?"

"Oh, it's not all that bad." Lily stepped forward. "We got it out here, certainly a strapping man like you can get it in the car for us."

Cyrus reddened slightly and grabbed it again. Lily grabbed the handle. "How 'bout you come in through the car, Cyrus and I'll tip it from over here? It'll slide in right slick that way."

Cyrus straightened up and crossed around behind the Buick, opened the door and laboriously crawled in the back seat. He grabbed the corpse again and pulled as Lily tipped.

The late Ricky Haverill slid into the back seat and farted audibly.

Cyrus jumped as the women's jaws hit their chests.

Betty slapped her hands to her cheeks. "Oh Cyrus!"

Cyrus straightened up, backing away from the car his cheeks flaming. "That weren't...that wasn't ME!"

Lily glared at Betty.

There was a moment of silence.

"That...that was ME." Rita timidly broke the silence.

"Oh, oh! Ha ha ha! I told you it wasn't me!" Cyrus backed away, his cheek still flame red, slapping his thigh. "I'm glad you said something Rita, because I was starting to think your 'rug' was actually a body, ha ha ha!"

Doris swallowed with a throat that was suddenly dry and closed shut.

The women snuck horrified looks at each other.

Lily recovered first, stepping forward and closing the rear door with a bang. "Thank you kindly, Cyrus. Next time, we'll call Goodwill to come get stuff like this. Say, you have any extra cream with you today?"

Cyrus closed the door of the Buick on his side and stepped back, his face cooled to his normal hue again. "Why yes, Miz Lily, I believe I do."

Lily crossed around the car and took his arm. "Wonderful. Can you leave me two pints with our order today then?"

Cyrus started the wheezing motor of his truck. "I'll put 'em all on the back porch. Say, you ladies need help with anything else before I go?"

Doris shook her head vehemently, "NO, I mean, no, thank you Cyrus. That's very kind of you."

Cyrus nodded once, satisfied, then fixed a stare on Rita. "You know, I used to have that same, er, issue that you've got. My doctor recommended bicarbonate soda, and it cleared it right up. You might want to try it." He shifted the truck into drive and rattled around the corner of the house to the back porch.

Rita had both hands clasped over her mouth, her face crimson. "Oh! Oh! He thinks...he really thought... oh my!"

Betty patted her arm. "Never mind that Rita. That was good thinking on your part. Come on, let's get back inside before he comes back through and decides to chat some more."

Lily patted Rita's other arm as they clambered back up the stairs. "That was a great save just now but...you know, maybe you OUGHT to try that bicarbonate of soda. Because you can do far louder than THAT!"

Chapter Seven

"Oh, my land." Doris slumped down into the sofa with a sigh. "I can't believe this." She rubbed her face.

Lily paced around the room as Rita and Betty took their customary spots on the couch and the recliner, respectively.

"Doris, WHAT are we supposed to do now? I know no one wants to hear this, but he IS going to start to stink, and soon. We don't have a lot of time. And now he's in our car!" Lily said.

"I know, I know, for heaven's sake, do you think I don't know that?" Doris leaned forward holding her head in her hands.

The women fell silent. They weren't used to seeing her rattled.

Doris sat upright again. "We will go get some ice, that's what. We will pack him in ice, as much ice as it takes. Rita, where does he live?"

Rita frowned. "He lives in Texas."

"TEXAS?!" Doris was aghast. "I thought you said he was heading to Washington, D.C.?"

"He is. There's an event there this weekend. But he was heading to a hotel, the Capitol Something-or-other. The article said his wife would be joining him for the fundraiser at the hotel."

"Oh, my land." Doris closed her eyes.

"You know, maybe a hotel is better, anyway." Betty chimed in. "It's GOT to be easier to get into than a private home. And someone this important, I'm SURE he must have security everywhere."

Doris fixed a steel gray-eyed glare on her. "And did he happen to have security around him last NIGHT, Betty? Because if anyone was with him at the Legion Hall, we are well and truly in a pickle!"

"Well, no, I mean, nothing that I saw anyway."

"So much for your 'he's so important' theory then." Rita snippily said.

"Well, I think this is good news, for us anyway." Lily said brightly. "If there's no security, and if he is supposed to be at a hotel, that means we might have the week to get him down there. If we can keep him from stinking. And speaking of that, you DO know that we will need to take the car to go get ice, right? The car with the late Ricky Haverill in it I might add."

"Oh ick!" Rita exclaimed.

"Oh no, no no no, count me out!" Betty stood up and started backing away. "I'm not doing that!"

"Oh my land." Doris closed her eyes as exhaustion hit her.

Lily shook her head and stood up. "You ladies obviously never lived on a farm. Death is a part of life. Rita, give me the keys. I'll go take care of this."

"Thank God!" Betty sank back into her chair.

Lily rolled her eyes and took the keys from Rita's quivering outstretched hand. "Let me get my bag. Betty, make sure you bring in the milk and eggs Cyrus left in the box. I'd hate to lose a week's worth over this."

She tromped out of the room. A moment later the sound of the Buick starting came through the air. The tires crunched then silence.

On the far wall, the clock ticked loudly as the hand crept toward 7:00 a.m. Sunlight painted patterns on the wall beside it.

The quiet in the room was dense and comforting.

Doris leaned back as a wave of exhaustion hit her. First the noise Betty had been making and then this. She closed her eyes. Just for a moment she thought.

Soon quiet snores began to fill the air.

The hands on the clock had reached 11:53 a.m. when a loud pounding broke the peace.

"Wha...what?" Doris jerked awake, disoriented. Across the room, Rita and Betty were similarly roused, blinking and foggy. Doris looked at the clock on the far wall. "My land! It's almost noon!"

The pounding started again.

"Who is that?" Rita whispered her eyes wide.

Betty shook her head mutely.

"No idea." Doris said as she stiffly pushed herself upright.

The pounding started again. Thud, thud THUD. Thud, thud, THUD.

"Well isn't THAT rude!" Doris had steeled her spine.

"Doris!" Rita gasped, "What if it's the Secret Service?"

"What?!"

"I mean, what if he DID have security last night and Betty didn't notice them?"

"Oh my land! Where's Lily? And where did she park the car?"

Thud, thud THUD. Then, "Miz Winslow? Miz Harris? Miz Tiernan? Miz O'Donnell? You ladies alright in there? I can hear you, you know."

"It's Officer Pim!" Rita hissed.

"Oh no!" Betty shrank back into the chair.

"I'll handle this!" Doris stood tall. "You ladies listen to me; Keep. Your. Mouths. Shut! Better yet, go upstairs. And look out for Lily. I don't know if she's back yet or not. She should be, it's been 5-hours."

Jim shouted through the door again. "If'n you all don't answer the door, then I'm coming in, because I cain't tell if you're okay or not."

"Hang on!" Doris shouted. "We aren't decent!"

"Oh geeze." came from the other side of the door. "Sorry about that."

Doris shuffled across the room to the foyer, noticing how disarrayed it looked from Ricky's unceremonious departure. She kicked a crumpled floor mat back into place and righted the vase that had toppled on her Queen Anne side table. Gingerly patting her hair, she opened the front door a crack.

Lieutenant Jim Pim's bright blue eye peered in at her. Standing well over 6-feet tall, he was a large, former farm boy turned cop. Doris knew him well, had had him in sixth grade like so many of the other police officers from the tiny Brownville P.D. A couple of years back he had hooked up with Sandy Case, a former big city reporter who had ended up in Brownville. Doris was happy for them both, and proud of what Jim had become.

She just wasn't all that thrilled at seeing him on her doorstep on this particular day.

Jim frowned at her through the small crack she had allowed. "Miz Winslow, you think you could open this door for me? I got to talk to you all about something, especially to Miz O'Donnell."

Doris stiffened, momentarily speechless. "Um. We aren't decent and I think Betty is asleep. She's got a cold. Hold on a minute while I get some clothes on."

"But you're WEARING clothes now, ma'am..." Jim's words were muffled as Doris slammed the door in his face.

She wheeled to face Betty and Rita. "Get her upstairs and in bed RIGHT THIS SECOND!" she muttered. "Betty, under NO circumstances are you to talk to Jim or anyone else!"

"Miz Winslow! Come on now! Open this door!"

"Go!"

Betty jumped up and scurried for the rear staircase.

"Hold your horses!" Doris shouted. She cast around for something else to put on, opening the closet where she tugged her winter coat out. She shimmied into her burgundy, knee length quilted coat and pulled it together across her ample bosom.

Taking a deep breath, she opened the door to a suspicious Jim. "I had to get dressed." She told him.

Jim stood on the front porch, his officer's hat in his hands. His eyes widened when he saw Doris clad in a down filled winter coat on this warm morning.

"Ma'am.... are you okay?"

Doris fluffed the faux fur collar around her neck. "I've taken a chill. And Betty is in bed with it. She can't speak to you at the moment."

Jim ran a hand over his short blonde hair, ruffling it up. "Well, Miz Winslow, can I come in for a moment then and talk to you?"

Doris hesitated, her eyes darting around the yard. The Buick was nowhere to be seen. Just Jim's cruiser, which was parked down on the street.

Just then, Carl Mannion cruised by, peering intently up the sidewalk at the house. Doris realized the cruiser was stirring up interest in them, interest she could certainly do without.

Reluctantly she opened the door wider. "Come in then. But only for a moment. We aren't well."

"I'll make it quick, ma'am."

Jim stepped through the opening. Doris slammed the door shut behind him.

"Well, what is it then?" she snapped, in her best sixth-grade teacher's voice.

Jim stiffened involuntarily at the tone.

"Ma'am, I need to know if Miz O'Donnell was here last night."

"Well of course she was here. She was right upstairs in her bed." Doris retorted, thinking well that's NOT a lie.

"Was she gone last night at all?"

"Now how would I know that? We don't watch each other's comings and goings. I know she was in her room, that I know, but when she went in there, well I can't help you with that."

Jim blew out his cheeks in exasperation. "Miz Winslow, can you help me out here? I got some people over at the station asking about Miz O'Donnell, or I should say, asking about your Buick. Their description of the driver sounded like Miz O'Donnell. I came over here instead of the Chief because I think it might go better here if'n we talk instead of him and those men."

"Wha...what men are those?" Doris asked with a mouth that was suddenly dust dry.

"Some kinda Washington D.C. types. They didn't really identify themselves but they came by just now askin' about the Buick and about Miz O'Donnell, or someone who looks an awful lot like her. They wouldn't say why only that it was mighty important that they have a word or two with her."

He craned around. "Where is your car, anyway?"

Doris felt like she was going to faint. Black spots danced in front of her eyes. She staggered slightly and reached for the newel post at the end of the staircase to steady herself. Jim jumped forward, catching her arm.

"Ma'am, are you alright?"

The heavy winter coat had given her a sheen of sweat across her face. "I...I told you; we aren't well! There's sickness in this house! Now I can't speak for Betty, but we heard her in her room last night, so those men must be mistaken. Surely there's other cars like ours around."

"Ma'am there aren't too many 1987 Buick LeSabre Limited's in this area." He replied dryly.

Regaining her composure, Doris straightened up and wiped a hand across her forehead.

"Well, I am sorry. I can't help you. You'll just have to come back tomorrow or another day then." She shuffled over to the front door and opened it. "Good day, Officer Pim."

"Ma'am, come on now. You know I wouldn't be here if'n it wasn't important."

"If it wasn't important, not 'if'n.' I taught you better than that, James Pim."

He flushed a deep shade of red.

"Yes ma'am. I'll be going then. But I will be coming back and I will be talking to Miz O'Donnell."

Doris nodded impatiently, "Yes, yes I know. Good day." She shoved the front door open wider.

Jim slapped his hat on his head and stomped out the door with a mutter.

Doris slammed the door shut behind him.

As he tromped down the front stairs, Doris saw a flash of dull blue coming down the road from the left.

She peered through the sidelight and her heart stopped.

Lily was steering the Buick in a big arc into the base of the driveway. Jim saw her and changed his path from his car to across the lawn toward her. Truly faint now, Doris grasped the door jamb and stopped breathing.

She heard a rustling behind her.

"Is he gone yet?" Betty asked.

Rita pulled the curtain over the window in the parlor to one side and exclaimed, "Oh! Oh no!"

Doris waved her hand violently. "Shhhhhh!" She pulled the door open a couple of inches and watched through the opening.

Lily halted the car and cranked the window down with a big smile. "Afternoon, Jim. How's your mom doing?"

"Oh she's doing alright, doing okay...say I gotta ask you..."

"Did she take up with the fair committee again? My land have we missed her apple pies at the sale."

"I, uh, I guess so, say Miz Harris, I gotta ask you something here." Jim hooked his two thumbs in his belt and squared himself up. Lily tilted her head and looked at him over her glasses.

"Uh oh. Now Jim, I know how proud you are of the Brownville Police Department and all, but I can't donate to the Policeman's Ball this year."

"Wait...what? No! No ma'am, that's not what I'm out

here for, no sir. Look Miz Harris, the boss got some Secret Service types asking about this here car, and about Miz O'Donnell too. You care to tell me WHY he'd be getting inquiries like that, ma'am?"

Lily regarded him with her lips pursed. "Why, I don't rightly know, son. Maybe they want to buy the car?"

"Buy the...buy the car? Now why in tarnation would they want to do something like THAT?" A flush was working its way up Jim's neck.

"Why maybe to haul one of those important people around in it. I mean look at it." Lily waved her hand encompassing the Buick from nose to tail. "Why it's such a fine machine, you could carry a half-dozen people in it. Why just LOOK at how large the back seat is!"

Doris, Rita and Betty gasped.

"Oh no...no, no, no, no! Lily! What are you doing?" Doris whispered.

Jim looked at Lily skeptically but stepped forward and peered into the back seat.

"Oh no! We're sunk!" Rita hissed.

Jim stepped back and regarded Lily with mild exasperation. "It's a mighty fine car and all, but I still don't know why they're interested in this car and in Miz O'Donnell. Where was she last night, ma'am?"

Lily snorted. "She was up in her room. We all heard her. What a racket she was making!"

Jim stepped forward with interest. "What? Why was she making a racket?"

"Well, because she was having sex."

"She was? Ma'am, if'n you don't mind me asking, who did she have in there with her last night?"

"Why Frankie of course."

Doris slapped her hands over her mouth."

"Frankie? Frankie who?"

Lily sniffed and regarded Jim over her glasses again. "Frankie the Dildo, Officer Pim. She was making on heck of a racket with that thing, buzzing until all hours of the wee morning. None of us slept a wink, I tell you!"

Jim stared at Lily, his jaw hanging. "Frankie the...surely you don't mean one of them...um... those...I mean..."

"Why I most certainly do! She keeps this up we're gonna have to get her a deep cycle marine battery, because she's going to go broke buying all of those double A ones, you know."

Jim's face was an interesting shade of bright scarlet. He started backing away from the car. "I...uh...I mean. Um, okay ma'am. You have yourself a nice day now." He spun on his heel and headed down the driveway for his car at what looked suspiciously like a trot.

Lily smirked after him then put the car in drive and continued up the driveway beside the house.

Doris pushed the door shut and leaned her head against it.

"Oh my.... oh my God!" Rita exclaimed.

Beside her, Betty looked thoughtful. "You think those can run off those big batteries like that?"

Doris pushed herself upright and started fumbling for her coat, stripping it off with shaking hands. "Why in the world didn't he react to Ricky's body in the back seat?" She spun and started shuffling through the house toward the kitchen. Rita and Betty trailed behind her.

Lily was closing the driver's door when the three women pushed their way onto the back porch. She turned and smiled brightly at them.

"Well, HE couldn't get out of here fast enough now, could he?" She chuckled.

Doris hobbled painfully down the steps and shuffled over to the rear door on the car. "Did you get the ice? Why were you gone so long? I can't believe Jim didn't say anything about...." She trailed off.

The rear seat was empty.

Lily smiled triumphantly. "Ice wasn't going to work, so I took care of it."

"What? What did you do?"

"Well, I went up to town to try and get some ice, and I thought to myself, 'Lily,' I said to myself, 'If you walk into the Co-Op or to the A&P grocery store or pert near any store here and buy 25 bags of ice, people are gonna remember that, yes sir.' So, I decided to go to each place and only get five bags."

Doris, Betty and Rita stared at her. Doris interjected, "How did you go from buying five bags per store to an empty back seat?"

"I went into the convenience store over on High Street first and guess who I ran into? Hiram."

Hiram was Lily's nephew. And he was also quite strange.

"What does Hiram have to do with this?" Doris asked in a faint voice.

"Well, you all know he's a big hunter and outdoorsman. He's also right handy with taxidermy now too, fact he started his own business with it last spring."

"Taxidermy?" Betty squeaked.

Doris's face had paled to the color of fine linen. "Please say you didn't...please say you didn't..."

Lily looked at her bright eyed. "Why yes, I did! Think about it: there's no way at all ice was going to keep that poor man for five, six days. But with taxidermy, why old Ricky will keep forever!"

The ladies stared at her with horrified expressions. Doris found her tongue first. "Lily! What in God's name are you thinking? You can't taxidermy a corpse!"

"Well, there aren't any laws against it in the books."

Rita spoke up in a faint voice, "You mean you can taxidermy your aunt Zelda or your husband and it's legal?"

Lily nodded. "Course you can."

Doris grasped her nose. "Lily, the last time I knew, it took months, YEARS even to get something taxidermized. It's not a fast process! We don't HAVE months or years! We have forty-eight hours, tops, before we have to leave."

"Don't you worry about a thing. Hiram knows that. He told me that because there isn't much hair on Ricky that he can speed cure the hide and even better: he won't have to use his skeleton because he has this slick articulated frame he can use instead. Old Ricky's gonna be able to stand, sit, lie down, anything we need him too. He wasn't gonna be able to do that all stinky and stiff."

"Oh my God." Rita covered her face with both hands.

"What about his skull?" Betty piped up. "Isn't he going to have to use that? Otherwise, Ricky won't look like Ricky."

Lily nodded. "Hiram said he's got it all figured out. Don't you worry. That boy's smart."

Doris glared at Lily. "That 'boy' is not all there either, Lily. What were you thinking? We can't have that man taxidermized!"

"Well...it's kinda too late now." Lily muttered.

"Well STOP him! When did you leave him there?"

"Oh, hours ago. He was already gutting him when I left."

"Gah!" Rita whirled and started retching into the bushes.

Doris staggered back a step and sank into the wicker chair next to the back door.

"We're done. That's it. We're all going to prison now."

Lily made her way up the steps to the porch. "Now Doris, how about you have some faith? Just give Hiram some time to get it done. He's right sure he can have Ricky back to us in forty-eight hours, or maybe even less than that."

Betty pouted slightly. "So, will he be able to move once he's all done up? Like we can move ALL of him?"

Rita whirled on her. "Betty, don't you even THINK about it!"

Doris fixed Lily with a steel gray-eyed glare. "Forty-eight hours Lily. Forty-eight hours TOPS or YOU'RE going to be the one going to the police about this!"

"Hey!" Lily was stung. "I'm not the one who brought him home to die here!" She glared at Betty.

"No, but YOU are the one who left him to be gutted and stuffed. Forty-eight hours, Lily."

Chapter Eight

"We have to act normally." Doris paced around the large sunny kitchen. "We can't let anyone think anything is wrong."

The ladies fell silent. Doris looked around the kitchen, the kitchen she had called her home for almost six decades now. Sunlight slanted across the room, highlighting the warm butcher block counter, gleaming on the copper pans hanging above it.

Over the kitchen sink, cuttings from various houseplants (Betty's specialty) glowed an almost incandescent green in the early afternoon light. The mullion paned windows threw sparks of blue and gold coloring onto the floor, a result of the light bending as it passed through the multifaceted edges of the glass.

It all looked so...normal...so far removed from the shenanigans of the previous night.

She pictured the scene the way it would look right now had they called the police last night. There would be men tromping through her house with big boots on, white Tyvek clad forensic specialists, and noise, noise, noise. Reporters clustered on the front yard, police coming and going and curious passerby's everywhere.

Then there was the matter of the Secret Service and maybe the F.B.I. or the C.I.A. or any number of alphabet soup agencies. She suddenly had a vision of herself sequestered in one of the empty rooms upstairs, being questioned over and over by men in black suits with earpieces. There may have even been dark helicopters thumping in the brilliant sky overhead, their blades whipping the fallen leaves into a frenzy.

Doris rubbed her suddenly damp forehead. They had to stay the course. As hard as this was, and would be, the other option meant suicide for the life they led now.

A life she was rather fond of.

She cast her gaze around the room at the other women, women she thought of as her 'family' now that she no longer had any.

Lily had crossed to the sink and was washing her hands, her once dark brown hair cropped short now and streaked with gray. Black rimmed glasses perched somewhat crookedly on her face; her frame was somewhat stout but strong, capable. Short fingernails spoke of hands that worked rather than hands that languished. She had dressed in a pair of jeans and a flowered tee shirt this morning; her feet clad in dark green Crocs. She had married a dairy farmer and lived as his wife for almost half a century before finding him dead in the milking parlor one morning, felled when his big heart had beat its last beat.

With just the one daughter living on the West coast, she had joined the small band of women here some two years ago now rather than uprooting and moving to Bellevue, Washington where her daughter lived.

She never spoke of it, but Doris knew she still struggled with the sudden changes in her life.

Rita had stopped pacing and was leaning against a counter, her left hand at her mouth, the knuckle of that thumb in it. Absently she chewed at it, a lifelong habit when she was stressed. She had removed the rollers from her hair and brushed it into dark waves that framed her face. An emerald cardigan covered her upper body; black pants clad her lower body. She still dyed her hair, still dressed smartly and kept herself as trim and fit as age and gravity would allow.

She and her husband Ron had not had children, had wanted them, but it was never to be. Rita had thrown herself into her bookkeeping career instead.

That ended up being her salvation when Ron had that massive stroke and died some ten years back now. Three weeks he spent in a coma, Rita at his side the entire time. He never regained consciousness.

Rita had held out for three more years on her own before answering Doris's ad one spring morning, about the open room.

By the time they had looked at the room, she was already one of their own.

And then there was Betty.

Oh Betty.

Doris looked across the sunny kitchen at Betty and felt a deep pang in her heart.

Betty was an 'it' girl, always had been, but carried it off unconsciously, with no airs, no drama.

Well, that is, if you ignored the sudden increase in wanton sex and one-night stands.

Her hair brushed her shoulders in platinum waves, the kind of color that looked more blond than gray. High cheek bones framed an arresting face, one that was punctuated by light brown eyes the color of amber. She was still willowy and youthful in looks...and lately, in actions too. Wearing faded jeans, scuffed riding boots and a white blouse open in a V at her neck, she looked like the kind of woman whose poster would have graced the walls in a 1970s era bedroom.

Doris thought of the signs that had been there for a while now, subtle, but there. The forgetfulness. The impulsiveness. The times she told the same story to them with no realization that she had just told it fifteen minutes earlier. The blank look she sometimes had when they were having conversations.

Oh, Doris knew about those signs, knew them well.

When you looked back to how she had been twelve years ago, when she moved in and compared it to now, the changes were obvious.

Betty had lived the life once, lived it well too. Married to Brad, a local politician just out of college, she had been the perfect wife during his brief upward trajectory.

Brad would end up being husband number one, his life cut short some forty-five years ago when a drunk crossed the line one rainy night, hitting him head on.

Betty had mourned him, mourned him hard.

Then she met Jon. Jon was handsome, charismatic, charming and a serial philanderer.

It was the oldest story in the book. Betty was the last to know. She didn't know during their courtship, didn't know during their engagement, didn't know the night of their lavish country club wedding, even when he was screwing that red-haired server in the stairwell behind the kitchen as the band played in the opulent ballroom.

She didn't know when she was married to him, didn't

know when she appeared on the pages of the local society news.

Didn't know on the night some five years into her marriage when a strange red-headed woman with a small boy in tow showed up on the front steps asking for her.

By the time the woman left, she knew.

The fallout was nuclear in its intensity. Because there were other things that neither Betty nor Miranda (the red-head) knew, namely that Jon was broke and also that he happened to still be married to wife number one. Two wives ago.

Betty was left penniless; Jon had already helped himself to her assets early on in the marriage. She had tried to carry on as best she could, but Jon's infidelities and his plain old theft from her had cut deep. Used to a certain kind of lifestyle, she had silently suffered as she lost piece after piece of it as the years marched on.

The day her home was foreclosed on was the lowest day of her life.

When she had shown up at Doris's back steps that day, she was one step away from desperation.

Doris had felt her pain and felt rage on her behalf.

That day, Betty became part of their little family.

The graceful old mansion the women occupied was usually home to up to eight women. In recent months, the move of Elizabeth and Connie to nursing homes, then Grace to her daughter's home in Michigan and Marilyn to Rhode Island with her son meant they had an unusually large number of empty rooms available.

And it also meant Doris felt the loss of her small family clan keenly. The house felt empty and just a little bit cold with so many empty chairs.

They had to be picky about who they chose to live with

them. Doris was the owner of the home, and she had decided long ago it was better to make it a co-op where ladies of her age could live out their lives gracefully.

Never did she imagine that would involve dead men and dildoes that needed deep cycle marine batteries.

She shook her head. They really needed to sit Betty down. She liked her, loved her even, had lived with her a long time, but this was too much. She had watched her mother go through it with her father; she wasn't going to bury her head in the sand any longer.

Doris herself had suffered too much loss to be willing to accept any more. She too had been married and had stayed married for 48 years. Her husband Walter had been a kind man, if a slightly boring one. Theirs hadn't been a marriage of passion; it was more like a business arrangement. But it was an arrangement that worked and worked well. Their affection for one another wasn't fake, her grief at his passing was real.

For decades, surrounded by children while in the classroom, she was secretly glad when there were none of their own. Children were...messy and complicated. And Doris didn't like mess and complications.

She liked things predictable and logical.

Which was the antithesis of her current situation.

Casting a look around the room, she repeated herself, "We have to act normally, but we can't be going out and gallivanting around. There's too much risk that people will start talking to us and one of us might say something we shouldn't."

"You already told Officer Pim Betty was sick." Rita interjected.

"I know. At least Betty can stay out of sight for the next

forty eight hours without too many people asking questions." She leveled a stare at Betty.

"Hey! What if I don't want to? I had things to do."

"I think you already did them Betty." Lily said drolly.

Betty blew her cheeks out in a pout. "You're just jealous."

Lily frowned. "But what about the groceries? I was going to head over to the A & P today to get this week's groceries. We surely can't stay here without food, Doris."

"Well why on EARTH didn't you do that earlier, then? Where were you for five hours, Lily? We have a crisis on our hands here in case you hadn't noticed."

"Geeze, relax Doris. I was at Hiram's giving him a hand. Rick wasn't exactly a small man, you know. It's gonna be fine. Hiram is a clever boy. If he says he can do this, he can do this. And you yourself are saying we have to act normal; well it doesn't get much more normal than doing our weekly shopping over at the market."

Doris leaned her elbows on the kitchen island and pinched the bridge of her nose. She took a deep breath. "Fine. Fine. Go do the shopping but get right back here." She straightened up. "Rita, do you have a list going?"

"Yes...yes of course. It's right here in the pantry."

She turned to walk across the kitchen.

DING-dong.

The women jumped and gasped in unison as the doorbell pealed through the house.

"Who is that?" Betty hissed at Lily.

"I don't know! Does it look like I have x-ray vision?"

DING-dong!

"Don't answer it!" Rita whispered. "What if it's the Secret Service out there?"

"Oh...oh no! Don't say it! Don't even think it!" Betty looked like she was going to faint.

"Shhhh!" Doris's shush cut through the room, perfected from years of refining it on 11-year-olds.

The women fell silent.

DING-dong DING-dong DING-dong!

"Oh, for Pete's sake!" Lily squared her shoulders, that stubborn look she was famous for gleaming in her eye. "I'll go deal with this!"

She shouldered the swinging door open and stomped out of the room.

"Lily! Lily, NO!" Doris stage whispered.

The door swung gently in its frame.

"Oh no, no, no, no! What if it's the CAI?" Betty squealed.

"CAI? There's no such thing as the CAI." Rita replied.

"Yes there is! We were watching that show just the other night, the one about the assassin, and he was fighting the CAI."

"It's the CIA." Rita corrected her. "That stands for Central Intelligence Agency. CAI would be Central Agency Intelligence. That just doesn't make any sense."

"Well Central Intelligence Agency doesn't either! You really think there's intelligence in an agency?"

"Ladies!" Doris hissed through clenched teeth. "Shut. Up!"

From the other room they could faintly hear Lily's voice, but not what she was saying. Doris closed her eyes as another wave of faintness hit her.

Maybe she really was getting sick.

Then...Lily's voice grew louder...she was coming back to the kitchen, and she was still talking to the agents...it HAD to be agents looking for Ricky Haverill...no one rang the front doorbell here when they knew them...and there was a strange shuffle-shuffle thud...shuffle shuffle thud...coming with her.

They had to be bringing in equipment to question them with, a battery of lie detector tests and brain wave caps designed to see the lies they were spinning. Maybe before Lily dropped him off to be skinned and preserved, they might have stood a chance, but not now.

She raised a hand to her mouth as the kitchen door quivered then swung open revealing Lily. She was stepping through, looking over her shoulder at whoever was following her.

And impossibly...she was laughing.

She stepped into the kitchen and held the swinging door in for the person following her, but the space behind her head was empty.

They looked down.

The woman was impossibly tiny, impossibly frail, but she shuffled and pushed the walker along with a strength that was in denial with her appearance. Short, straight gray hair was brushed back off of a high forehead, round glasses twinkled as the sunlight hit them. She was clad in a gray sweater, a dark rose shirt and a brown knee-length skirt. Tennis balls cushioned the legs on her walker, dirty and scuffed from use. On one side, a messenger style bag swung, secured by twine.

The three women stared blankly at her.

Lily looked around the room, smiling brightly. "Ladies. This is Donna Green. She's here about the room."

Doris's legs gave out on her. With a strangled moan, she sank to the floor.

Chapter Nine

"I'm fine Betty! Will you stop fussing over me?" Doris waved her hands sharply at Betty and swung upright from the white framed day bed in the parlor where the women had deposited her after her unceremonious crash to the kitchen floor.

She looked across the room at Donna, who leaned on her walker looking around the room with unabashed interest.

The rooms. She had completely forgotten about the rooms for rent.

Lily pushed the swinging door open from the kitchen and set the tea pot and cups on the low table. "Here you go, Donna. Why don't you sit down over there?"

"Don't mind if I do. I've been on my feet a long time, you know." Donna shuffled over and sank slowly down into the green and pink ruffled recliner. She set her walker to one side with a thud and reached out to take the cup of tea Rita was offering. She raised it to her mouth with a palsied hand, the tea sloshing over the rim and dripping onto the carpet.

Rita's eyes were round.

Doris couldn't even react. The exhaustion of their circumstance and adventures had hit her hard. She stared mutely at Donna.

Lily glanced uncertainly at Doris then asked Donna brightly, "So Donna, it's so good to see you again. I think it's been, what, fifteen years or more since our paths crossed. What have you been up to?"

Donna set her cup down with a clunk, sloshing more tea over the rim. "What have I been up to? What have I been UP to? Why I've been up to getting old and disabled, that's what I've been UP to."

Betty rolled her eyes as Lily drew herself upright. "Well, you don't have to be snappy with me about it. I'm just being polite."

"Humph." Donna reached for the cup again. "I learned a long time ago that being polite is overrated. All you do is waste time with chitter chatter, 'Oh Donna, how ARE you? What a nice blouse you're wearing.' When what they REALLY want to say to you is, 'You're still alive? What a pity.' No, I don't place much stock in that sort of thing anymore."

She set the cup down haphazardly, more tea sloshing over the edge. "I'm here about the room. Tell me about that why don't ya?"

Lily looked to Doris for help, but Doris remained mute.

"Well," she started, "It's a large room on the south side, so it gets lots of sun. It has a bathroom of its own, and it's fully furnished. All utilities are included..."

"Where is it located?" Donna interjected. She craned her head around. "Is it off one of those rooms?" She gestured toward the dining room.

"No, no it's upstairs." Lily replied.

"Is there a stair lift here? I didn't see one when I came in. I can't do stairs like those anymore."

"N...no. We talked about getting one, but we don't have one yet."

"I thought you advertised this room as being disabled friendly?"

"Well, it IS. There's handles in the bathroom and the tub is a walk-in. But we don't have a stair lift here."

"Well, what the hell are you going to do when someone dies upstairs? Slide the body down the staircase like a bobsled? I mean, you're all a bunch of old ladies too; I'm sure if it hasn't happened yet that it's going to one day."

The women exchanged uncomfortable looks.

"That may be a more efficient way to move a corpse downstairs than a granny launcher would be, hypothetically speaking of course." Lily said dryly.

Donna snorted. "Well, I'd expect you to have one installed. You can't be calling yourself disabled friendly and not even have the most basic accommodation to it."

Doris sighed and replied, "I'll take it under advisement. They were outlandishly expensive, and we were all able to handle the stairs, so we didn't bother investing in one."

Donna set her tea back down with a palsied splash. "I would think you'd want one. You're all older than I am for Pete's sake. How much a month is this room, anyway?"

Doris told her.

She snorted. "Really? That much for a room? I'd expect that for an apartment, not a room! Why it would be like living in a college dorm again!"

"Hey, you have all the privacy you want in your room. We all do whatever we want in our own rooms, right Betty?" Lily had a small smirk visible as she said it.

Doris gritted her teeth. "We're just a group of women

trying to make it the best we can, Donna. We found out a long time ago that having a small community was better for all of us than living alone. We don't have all the bells and whistles a nursing home would have; it's just us looking out for each other."

Donna looked around the room, her glasses twinkling in the sunlight. "Well, what about laundry and housekeeping? Surely you don't expect us all to do that!"

Doris sat up and leaned forward, her elbows on her knees. "Donna, it's more than a room. We have a little... community...here and we help each other out. We all have different tasks we take care of. If one person can't do their share, it's an undue burden on the others."

"What, are you saying I won't pull my weight? Well, let me tell you this; I've worked all my life. I just need to... simplify things for a while. I can't take care of a home by myself anymore! I'll tell you what: I will pay you half of what you're asking, then when you get the lift installed, I'll pay the full price."

"Donna, I am sure you are lovely, but I don't think you'll be a good fit. We all have to get along here. There's no drama or conflict in this house and I am not about to introduce any."

"Humph. Well, that answers that then. Thanks for the tea. It's weak, by the way." She said to Lily.

She grasped her walker and hauled herself out of the chair.

There was a knock at the front door.

"Oh, for heaven's sake!" Doris exclaimed. Were they to have no peace at all on this terrible day?

Betty went to the door and opened it.

Jim Pim stood on the step with Brownville Police Chief Tony Santos. They wore stern expressions.

Donna thumped her way across the foyer and glanced at Doris with a sneer. "Glad there's no drama in THIS house. Ladies..." she nodded at Lily and Rita then pushed her way past the two officers. "You gents mind giving me a hand getting down those stairs? This household isn't as disabled friendly as they seem to think they are."

Jim took her elbow and steadied her as she carefully tottered down the steps.

Chief Santos pinned them with a look. "Ladies. May we come in for a moment?"

Doris stammered, "I...uh...we aren't well, gentlemen."

He looked down the sidewalk where Donna was shuffling to her car, Jim still at her elbow.

"You were well enough to entertain her."

"I don't think 'entertain' is the word I'd use for that old..."

"Lily!" Doris cut her off, "Don't speak ill of our guest!"

Jim rejoined them on the porch. "Ladies, we really need to talk. Especially to you, Betty."

"Me?" Betty placed a hand at her throat and preened visibly. "Why you know I always talk to the boys! Come in!" She waved a hand toward the parlor.

Doris stepped forward, "Now Betty, you aren't well, remember?" she hissed through clenched teeth. "Perhaps these officers should come back another day when you are yourself!"

"Oh I feel quite alright now! Come in, please do!" She smiled coquettishly at them. Jim flushed a dull red. "You're cute, you know that?" She giggled, leaning over toward him.

Chief Santos ignored the comment and strode into the parlor. He eyed the women with a stern look on his face.

"I hate asking this, but do you have anyone else here in this house?"

"Why, no, no we don't." At least that was true now, Doris thought as she said it. "It's just us ladies."

"Ma'am, I need to ask your permission to search this house for a man. We have a request to find someone and there's reason to believe he may be here."

Rita's face went pale.

"Well hell," Lily stepped forward. "We got nothing to hide, Tony. Come on, I'll walk you boys through." She stepped forward.

"Just me. Lieutenant Pim will stay down here with you ladies while we do a walk through. We'll be quick."

"Right this way then." Lily bustled out of the room and onto the polished staircase, the same one the late Ricky Haverill had slid head-first down mere hours ago. Chief Santos followed her up the stairs.

Jim stood near the parlor door to the foyer, his hands behind his back, looking ill at ease. He looked at the women and said, "I'm right sorry about this, ladies. But we have people asking questions that need answering. As soon as we are done, we'll be out of your hair."

"It's okay." Betty said as she sidled over next to Jim. His face turned a brighter shade of red as she ran her hand up his arm. "I can show you around upstairs if you want."

"Ma'am...ma'am, I, uh, no I have to stay down here with you." He pulled his arm away from her.

They settled into an uncomfortable silence. Betty stood close to Jim beaming up at his face. She reached up and rubbed his upper arm again. "Ooooo! You're strong!"

"Betty," Doris said, "Officer Pim here has a girlfriend. Leave him be now."

From upstairs there came a muffled exclamation, then footsteps pounding down the stairs. Chief Santos appeared, his face an interesting shade of dark red. "Lieutenant Pim!

Let's go. Sorry to bother you ladies. Good day!" He yanked the front door open and stumbled on the stoop in his haste to exit. With a puzzled look around the room at them, Jim followed the Chief down the stairs, almost running to catch up to him.

From the second floor came Lily's raucous laughter.

"Lily?" Doris turbo waddled to the bottom of the stairs, Rita and Betty at her heels.

Lily appeared at the top of the stairs holding that...that THING with both hands. She flicked a switch, and the buzzing started, amplified by the staircase.

"Frankie saves the day again!" she called, breaking into a belly laugh.

"Hey!" Betty yelled, "Be careful with that!"

"What...what..." Doris stammered, "Lily, turn that darn thing off! What happened?"

Lily flicked the switch off and regarded the device thoughtfully for a moment. "I still say I've seen horses with smaller ones." She set the device on the little telephone table in the alcove at the top of the stairs.

Doris shuddered. THAT was going to need a thorough cleaning now.

"Well, I walked Chief Santos through the rest of the rooms, and I was going to kind of, you know, just walk right on past Betty's room but he insisted on seeing that too. It's still pretty messed up in there, with all the bedclothes tumbled onto the floor. He looked at that and demanded to know if Betty had anyone over last night. When I asked him why he would think that he said it was because of how mussed the bed was." She smiled brightly. "So, I told him that Betty entertained Frankie last night." She started to chuckle, then bent over as the laughter bubbled out of her. Straightening up, she wiped tears from her eyes. "When I said that he got all excited like, 'Frankie? Frankie who? Is he here?' And I said, why yes indeed, he's RIGHT HERE! And I pulled Frankie out of her drawer and fired him up, kinda started waving him around at him like a light saber. That man turned pale like he saw a ghost and about ran outta the room. Heeeeeee!" She doubled over again. "I would have never thought the Chief of Police in Brownville, Vermont was afraid of a dildo."

"Frankie to the rescue!" Betty clapped her hands together. "Although I kinda wish that other officer hadn't left too. I was just getting to know him."

Doris groaned, pressing her fingertips to her forehead.

Forty-eight hours, well forty-three now.

It felt like a lifetime.

Chapter Ten

"Has he called yet?" Doris fidgeted and moved her tea cup from one side of the table to the other. Outside the day hung low, soft, gray and damp. She glanced up at the kitchen clock; 3:30 p.m.

"Relax. It hasn't even been thirty six hours yet. He'll do it." Lily beamed, confidence brimming from her.

Rita scowled. "You're pretty sure of yourself there, missy."

"I told you, that boy's clever."

"He can't be that clever; he agreed to gut and stuff the leading candidate for the Office of the Vice President of the United States. Has there been anything on the news about him yet?"

Betty set her cup down and wrapped her knee length woolen cardigan around her tighter. "I saw on this morning's news that reporters were asking where he is, and that his office is saying he is taking some time off before next weekend. They MUST know he's missing!"

Rita pursed her lips. "With all this fussing about the

stuffing, we haven't talked about what we do AFTER he's mounted."

"Oh, Rita! That's rather...inelegant." Doris shuddered.

"Well, she has a point, you know." Lily said, "What are we supposed to do with him once we get him back?"

"Why take him to Washington, D.C. of course." Doris replied.

"Can't we just send him by train?" Betty wanted to know.

"No...no. We will have to take him by car. He should fit in the trunk." Doris replied hesitantly.

"The trunk?" Rita stared at her, one brow arched. "The trunk? Doris, you DO remember how much Mr. Haverill weighed, don't you?"

Betty was frowning. "I don't like that plan."

"Well, I haven't heard anything better from you!" Bright red spots bloomed on Doris's cheeks.

"Listen up ladies. We have to have a plan here. IF Hiram comes through, we have to be ready to leave as soon as he gets back to take him down to Washington, D.C."

"He'll come through." Lily interjected. "When Hiram gives you his word, it's good."

"Too bad his word didn't also include thinking things through, like agreeing to taxidermy the leading candidate for the Vice Presidency of the United States of America!" Doris's temper was starting to slip.

Lily sniffed and folded her arms. Betty cast a nervous glance at her then asked timidly, "What do you mean WE have to take him to Washington? Can't you and Lily or Rita take him instead?"

Doris fixed a laser glare on her. "From this point forward, we stick together. NO ONE will be left behind. If anyone stops in and asks any more questions, we can't risk having Lord knows what being said." She shook her head, a dogged expression on her face. "No. We need to plan now. All of you get your overnight bags and only pack enough for four days tops. Pack light, re-wear clothing if you have to. We'll hide our bags in the garage. Once it...he is back, we wait for nightfall and casually drive on out of here."

Rita frowned. "Are you sure we can manage driving all the way down to Washington by ourselves? That means driving through New York City and New Jersey."

"Ick." Lily and Betty replied in unison.

Doris closed her eyes briefly as a headache started pounding slowly.

"It's not like we can call Uber for a corpse you know. So, until then we act like nothing it wrong, that everything is normal, do you understand?"

They fell silent for a moment.

"This is awful!" Betty's lower lip was protruding, the way it did when a meltdown was imminent. "I've been stuck in this house since Sunday night! I had to cancel my hair appointment!

"Now I don't want to hear anymore about being 'stuck' in this house. Maybe if you had been a little more 'stuck' last Sunday, we wouldn't..."

The rapping on the back door made everyone jump.

"Oh my LAND!" Rita exclaimed.

Doris swallowed, her mouth suddenly dry. Betty was closest to the back porch. She teased the curtain on the window up an inch, peering cautiously through the crack.

"It's a woman." She whispered.

The rapping came again.

Doris took a deep breath and stood up from the kitchen

table. Tugging at the hem of her sweater, she reached out and unbolted the lock and opened the door a couple of inches.

A pair of bright, beady eyes peered back in at her.

"Good afternoon! I'm here about the room."

Wrinkles appeared between Doris's eyes. "I...I wasn't expecting anyone."

"Oh, I know that, Doris. I thought I'd just pop by on my way home today."

"Dana? Is that you?" Betty cautiously edged over to the door.

"Betty! I was hoping to see you!" Dana Oakes, one of the columnists over at the Brownville Reporter, pushed the door with her palm, opening it another six inches. "You're just the person I wanted to see!"

"I thought you said you were here about the room?" Doris tried vainly to push the door back.

"I am, I am...I want to write about you ladies in my next column. And I especially want to interview Betty!"

Rita stared at Dana like she had seen a ghost as Betty preened.

"Why...why do you want to talk to Betty?" she gasped.

"Oh you know, this and that. We go way back, don't we Betty? Way back indeed." Dana smiled, an empty one that fell short of her eyes. "Why I used to write about you all the time when you were married to Jon."

Betty flushed. "I'd rather not talk about him, thank you."

Dana gave the door another shove, allowing her to sidle sideways into the kitchen. She glanced at the table where the teapot and cups sat.

"Why I'd love a cup of tea! It's been so long. There's so much to catch up on here!"

She rummaged in the large brown and red bag that

hung from her left forearm, coming up with a leather clad notebook.

She pulled back a chair with a screech and deposited her rather large derriere in it.

"So, Betty. Care to tell me about Richard Haverill?"

The air left the room.

Dana looked around at the stunned women. "Oh, come on now. Did you really think you could keep a secret in a town this size? Why everyone knows the CIA has been seen in town. And that the police have been here twice in the past day. And that Betty here was the last person to be seen with Mr. Haverill. So. Where is he?"

Lily's eyes narrowed. "What are your sources, Dana? Do you really have nothing better to do than to harass us?"

"My sources are private." Dana replied archly.

"Mmm. And I am sure they are impeccable. Kind of like the time you wrote that story about the wife of the grade school principal having an affair, all because you saw her twice in Montpelier, only to find out she was undergoing stem cell therapy."

Dana flushed and muttered, "Well, we all make mistakes. Now Betty? Tell me about Richard Haverill."

Betty stared at her blankly. "Who?"

Dana snorted, "Who? What are you, an owl? You were SEEN with Richard Haverill last Sunday, Betty. And now the police have been coming by. Surely you must remember that!"

Betty looked at the floor, a furrow in her brow. "I remember the police. But I don't remember any man named Richard."

Doris looked sharply at her. Betty's eyes were genuinely bewildered.

Dana stared at her a moment, her frown deepening.

"Last Sunday? Over at the Legion Hall across the river? Sue Gantz and her husband were there. It was a campaign stop for Haverill, the last one before he was supposed to go back to Washington to join his running mate, Horace Rock. Only now," And here she fixed a beady eyed, piercing stare on Betty's face, "He's apparently missing. So give it up: are you two running away together? Or did you kill him and put him in mason jars in the basement?"

"Well, I can tell you THAT definitely didn't happen!" Lily chimed in.

Doris shut her eyes briefly as a massive headache bloomed behind them.

Dana Oakes was one of the last, if not THE last person she wanted sniffing around.

"So, what DID happen, Betty?" Dana pinned her down with her bright-eyed stare. "Where is Richard Haverill?"

"I don't know anyone named Richard Haverill, Dana." Irritation was creeping into Betty's voice. "And I don't think I want to be interviewed by you either!"

"Oh, come on. It's just between friends!" Dana stirred three lumps of sugar into her tea. Her pants rode a solid six inches up her ankles, revealing white socks and black flats. A purple cardigan strained to cover her white clad chest, curly brown hair in ringlets framed a face that was feral and calculating.

Doris stood up. "Dana, if you don't mind, it's too late in the day for this and we have things to do."

"What sort of things?" Dana asked slyly.

"Just...things...you know, we have people coming over to see the rooms, Lily still has to go do the shopping. Betty hasn't been well, so she will probably go back to bed. And Rita and I have to start dinner."

"We you can at least show me the room for rent then."

Rita eyed her narrowly. "Why? Your husband finally kick you out?"

"Oh, no no. I told Sue Coldwell that I would take a look at it for her. She's thinking about giving up that massive house."

The women exchanged uncomfortable looks.

"Okay, alright. Fine. Lily, would you mind giving our guest a quick look at the room? And then she really must be going." Doris fixed a stern look at Dana, who studiously ignored it.

Lily sniffed. "Fine. Come on then."

Dana pushed the chair back with another screech and gave Betty a piercing look. "If your memory comes back, you know how to reach me. Better me than any of those other reporters, the ones who don't know you or care about you."

Hoisting her bag, she trailed out of the room behind Lily.

"What are we supposed to do now?" Rita hissed.

"I don't know! Just...show her the room and get her the heck out of here!" Doris whispered.

"Who is Richard Haverill?" Betty asked in a normal voice. Rita and Doris stared at her. "You don't know?" Rita asked, "You really don't know?"

Betty shook her head no. "I know I've been sort of... forgetful lately, but I honestly don't know who that could be!"

Rita and Doris exchanged looks.

"He's no one, honey." Doris said. "Don't you worry about him."

Outside in the driveway behind the kitchen, a car horn

beeped. The women jumped. "Oh, my land. NOW what?" Doris moaned.

The horn blew again.

Doris and Rita crowded out onto the porch and peered out the back door.

Hiram Waller, Lily's nephew waved at them from inside his pickup truck.

Seated in the front seat with him was Ricky Haverill.

"Oh my God!" Doris covered her face with her hands.

From behind them in the house, they could faintly hear voices.

"This is a disaster!" Rita whispered.

"Why is he back so soon?" Doris's voice was faint.

Betty frowned at her. "You've been asking about when he would be here all day. Now you don't want him?"

"I wanted him to get back but NOT RIGHT NOW!"

Dana's voice echoed down the staircase. They had to be right at the top of it.

Doris shouldered the back door open. "Hiram Waller! You get that thing out of here right now!"

Hiram was tall and skinny, with sunken cheeks where teeth used to reside and dirty jeans that hung off lean hips. His blue ball cap was pushed back off his forehead and a tattoo crawled toward the light from the neck of his tee shirt.

His face was a study of bewilderment.

"But I thought you wanted him back right quick? Aunt Lily said so."

"But not right NOW!" Doris wrung her hands as sweat popped out on her forehead. "He can't be here!"

The voices in the house got louder. They were coming back to the kitchen.

Rita whirled around, her eye falling on the box of

discarded clothing and bedding they were supposed to donate. She pounced on the tattered old bedspread in teal and gray, pulling it free.

"Cover him up!" she thrust the comforter at an astonished Hiram. "Don't let Dana Oakes see him!"

"Oh geeze." Hiram said, "I didn't know she was here!" He snatched the comforter and wound it around the late Ricky Haverill.

Footsteps sounded from inside then the door opened revealing a scowling Dana Oakes and a nervous Lily. Her eyes darted to Hiram then to Dana. She looked back at the truck and blanched when she saw the corpse shaped thing swathed in the old comforter in the front seat.

Dana sniffed as she stomped down the stairs. She turned to Betty and wagged a finger in her face, "I'm going to find out what you've been up to. You know nothing gets by me in this Brown Town." She glanced over at Hiram, then at the bundle in the front seat. Her face registered no reaction. She looked back at Betty. "Consider yourself warned. Good day, ladies." Laboriously she made her way down the steps and waddled down the driveway toward the road.

"Well hell." Hiram said as she disappeared down the driveway.

Doris was almost hyperventilating.

"We have to get him under cover! NOW!"

"Doncha wanna see him first? He came out right good!" Hiram beamed.

Doris whirled on him. "I can NOT believe you agreed to this hare-brained scheme! Don't you know you just got us into all sorts of trouble doing this?"

"Hey, Aunt Lily said ya'll needed to take him home, and

that you didn't want him to start stinking. It's legal to taxidermy someone in this state."

"Yeah, maybe if you're his next of kin it is." Rita interjected dryly.

Hiram pushed his hat back on his forehead and stared dumbstruck at Lily.

"Wait...what? You said it was her cousin." He indicated Betty with his chin.

"Kissing cousin I guess." Betty said.

"Well shit!" Hiram shifted the plug of tobacco in his cheek and spat a brown stream at the truck's front wheel. Doris shuddered. "Aunt Lily! You done got me wrapped up in something I didn't know about! I ain't going to jail for this, am I?"

The women shared a look. Doris cleared her throat, which was suddenly dry. "Not if you don't say anything. We will keep it to ourselves. And we have to get him back to his family."

Hiram muttered a curse. "This was some of mah best work too! I'm right proud of how he came out."

Rita cast a nervous glance down the driveway. "Doris, don't you think we should get him into the garage and into the trunk? Quickly? Lord knows who else is going to show up next."

Lily turned to Hiram. "Will he go in the trunk of the Buick okay? He can be folded, right?"

"Folded? This here gentleman can sit, stand, bend, heck he can even do cartwheels if'n you need him to. I'm right proud of how he done came out. Come on; let's get him inside and I'll show you proper."

Lily and Rita hustled over to the garage and tugged the sliding door open. Betty peered in through the truck window at the shrouded Ricky Haverill. "I'm curious to see him again. You said I met him?" She looked at Doris with eyes clear of guile.

Doris felt the pang deep in her heart.

"Just for a moment, dear. I don't expect you would remember him."

Chapter Eleven

"Umph…." Hiram grunted as he muscled the corpse out of the truck's front seat. The legs were visible beneath the comforter, clad in slacks and bent in a sitting position. With a series of ratcheting clicks, Hiram straightened them and balanced Rick in an upright position.

He beamed. "It's a right shame I can't show him off. Check it out!" With a flourish, he tugged the comforter off, leaving it in a puddle on the ground.

"Ta da!"

The women gasped in unison.

"Oh my God!" Rita whispered.

Doris had staggered backward, her hand on her chest.

Betty backed up, her hands covering her mouth.

The man that stood before them resembled a man, but also didn't resemble one. He was leaner than the late Ricky Haverill, and about the same height. But there was something just…wrong…with him.

Lily frowned at it then stepped a bit closer. "What in tarnation is wrong with his eyes?"

"Oh, that." Hiram replied, somewhat sheepishly. "I didn't have no human type eyes..."

"Any." Doris replied automatically, her stare locked on the face of that...thing.

"ANY human eyes," Hiram continued, "So I had to make do with what I had. These here are bear eyes. Pretty neat, huh?"

"Oh, dear God." Doris muttered.

"That's just plain creepy." Rita said.

Betty frowned at the man in front of her. "I knew him?"

Ricky Haverill's face was his face, and it wasn't his face. Doris had only seen him after death, but she had to admit it only bore a fleeting resemblance to him, his features somehow uneven and out of proportion.

But worst of all, dear God, were the eyes. Where human eyes with round pupils and whites around them had once been were large, round brown eyes that filled the space. The pupils were round, but much larger than the average human. Ricky's hair had been brushed into some semblance of order by Hiram, but it still didn't look natural. She looked down at his hands.

He sported a pair of black gloves.

Hiram saw her looking and flushed. "His, ah, his hands didn't quite turn out the way I wanted 'em too, so I dug out a pair of old gloves for you."

Lily sized Ricky up and down and frowned at the car. "Doris, I don't think he is gonna fit in the trunk that easy. He's a right big man."

"NOW I remember him!" Betty beamed. "Ricky!" She caressed his arm, then frowned. "He feels kinda weird, like there's metal under this coat.

Hiram shuffled and looked at the ground. "I was in kind of a hurry, so I had to improvise. I managed to cure the skin right quick, but it shrank a little so I couldn't put any padding between the skin and the frame."

"Oh, ick!" Rita pursed her lips like she had tasted something rotten.

"Hey, he was going to start to stink, okay? Look we just need to get him down to D.C. and drop him off. Let them figure it out."

"D.C.? Like...Washington D.C.? What the hell did you get me into, Aunt Lily?" Hiram was staring at them with frank suspicion now.

"Nothing, Hiram. Don't you worry about that at all. As long as you say NOTHING to anyone everything will be alright, right ladies?" Doris sent a hard glare at the little group.

Lily looked at the late Ricky Haverill. "Well, let's figure out how we can get him into the car then. Hiram, give us a hand."

Doris rubbed her temples and stared at him. "Hang on a moment." She shuffled across the garage to the small storage room she kept off of it. There was rustling and crackling for a moment. She reappeared with a coat draped over her arm and a hat. "Let's put these on him first."

Hiram beamed. "Watch this! This is pretty neat!"

Carefully he articulated the arms, bending wrist and elbow to accommodate the coat. He slid the overcoat on him and adjusted the front.

Doris placed the hat, her husband's old fedora that went with his overcoat she had just sacrificed for the corpse, onto its head.

The little group fell silent studying it.

"That's still not right!" Rita broke the silence. "It's those darn eyes! We need sunglasses for him."

"Well you can't have mine!" Betty replied, "They're prescription and cost me a fortune."

"I don't have any." Lily said.

"Nor me." Doris interjected.

Hiram frowned. "I got a pair, but I'm kinda fond of 'em. Got them at the Daytona 500 a couple years back. I hate to give them up..."

"So go back next year and get a new pair." Lily told him. "Where are they?"

"In my truck." He shuffled out to the cab and rummaged on the dash for a moment.

"Here." He handed them over as he returned.

Lily held them out in front of her. "Well. I can see why you want to keep THESE." She looked at Hiram over the top of her glasses drolly.

The sunglasses sported red reflective lenses and large black frames with DAYTONA printed in white on the temple pieces and the number 8 printed on the corner of the left lens.

"Anything is better than these eyes!" Doris shuddered.

"Here." Rita snatched them out of Lily's hand and gingerly slid them onto the dead man's face.

They all stood and stared at the final effect a moment.

Ricky Haverill stood, or lurked really, with the too small overcoat brushing the tops of his thighs and the fedora covering his forehead. The sunglasses glowed in the dim light of the garage, the red garish against the blacks and grays he sported. The skin on his face was a ghostly white color, almost translucent.

Doris covered both of her eyes with her fingers as another headache blossomed.

"We should have just gotten the damn ice, Lily!"

"Well, it's too late now. Come on, Hiram. If he won't fit

in the trunk, then let's at least buckle him in back. Hey!" She looked up, a smile impossibly blossoming. "We can use that new carpool lane over by the airport now!" She cackled.

Rita rolled her eyes and Betty fidgeted.

"Just get him out of sight!" Doris snapped.

Hiram balanced Ricky and started ratcheting the arms and legs again, bending him into a seated position. "This here framework I made up has gears and bicycle chains to move the limbs around. I been working on this for a while but I hadn't done one yet. I was gunna use this one on that bear that Buck Checker brought me, but I guess I can make up another one. Still kinda sad I can't show this one off to anyone though."

"See? I told you he was clever." Lily said as she grasped a limb and started manipulating it. "Wow, that's easy to do too. You better patent this one, Hiram."

He beamed.

With some grunting and manhandling, they inserted Ricky into the back seat.

"Make sure you buckle him in!" Betty said.

They slammed the door shut and looked at him.

In the dim light of the garage, he could almost pass for being normal looking...if you didn't look too closely that is. The hat covered his upper half of the face and the glasses the middle.

Doris frowned, then opened the door again and raised the collar of the coat up so it shielded the lower part somewhat.

She shut the door.

"THAT doesn't look shady at all, now does it?" Rita said.

"You have a better idea?" Doris wheeled on her.

"I would have put him on the train and sent him out of here to someplace, anyplace." Rita answered.

"What ARE we going to do now?" Betty asked.

Doris shot a side glance at Hiram. "Why we are going to thank Hiram for his help and send him home, then we are going to get some dinner ready."

"Wait...I'm kinda hungry myself you know." Hiram protested.

Doris grasped his upper arm. "Young man. Thank you for all of your assistance. Now please leave. And unless you want to spend an uncomfortable amount of time talking to authorities, you're going to get yourself home and forget you ever did this."

"But what about my framework? I'm right proud of that one!"

Lilly patted his other arm. "Hiram, you come on by next week and I'll reimburse you for what you spent on that, okay?"

"You sure I ain't going to get in any kinda trouble here?"

Doris patted his arm and said in a voice that dripped steel. "As long as you keep your mouth shut, everything will be fine."

Chapter Twelve

Doris closed the kitchen door and sagged back against it. Her hips were screaming now. How dearly she wanted to just take a heating pad and settle down in the living room with a book!

"What do we want for dinner tonight?" Rita asked, "I'm not sure how much food we have."

Doris's eyes snapped open. "Rita! There's no time for that! Everyone! Go pack your clothes...NOW. Let's move! We need to be out of here as soon as it's dark! We will get something to eat along the way."

"Can't we wait and leave in the morning?" Betty wanted to know.

"No! The sooner we can get him out of our lives, the sooner we can get our lives back. Come on now! Let's move!" Wincing against the pain, Doris pushed herself upright again.

"Geeze, sometimes it's like being back in grade school." Lily muttered.

Betty's lower lip was protruding dangerously. "Well, I'm hungry! I've hardly slept nor eaten much today."

"Go! GO!!" Doris waved her hands vehemently. "Enough of the bickering!"

Betty snorted, but sullenly tromped away as she had been told, Lily and Rita in tow.

Doris rubbed her aching hip and slowly made her way toward the front staircase. She glanced up the gleaming sweep of the stairs with some trepidation.

Maybe there WAS some merit to having a chairlift installed.

As she grasped the railing, there was a rapping noise from the front door behind her.

"Oh, for the love of God!" she muttered savagely. She considered simply ignoring it and making her way up the stairs instead.

The rapping came again, louder, more insistent.

With a whispered curse that she had only heard her husband use twice in his life (and she, never) she whirled and yanked the door open.

"WHAT IS IT!" she shouted.

Donna Green stood on the porch, leaning on her battered walker. A frown line appeared between her eyes.

"Well that certainly isn't any way to greet someone!"

"It is if that person happens to be YOU! What is it now?"

She sniffed and shifted uncomfortably. "Well, I thought I'd give you a second chance, you know, after you were so rude and all."

"A second chance for WHAT?" Doris was incredulous.

"Why to get my business as a renter of course. You're not going to find a more suitable person, well as long as you uphold your end of the bargain."

"What bargain?" From upstairs, Doris was aware of the

sounds of thumping and drawers being open and closed as the women packed their bags.

"You installing that chairlift so that I can move around in comfort. And having someone come in for the heavy cleaning and laundry and so on."

"We don't HAVE a deal, Donna! That was YOU making demands of ME!" she rubbed her aching hip as she glared at the woman.

Donna looked past her at the broad expanse of stairs. "You mean to tell me you've NEVER considered installing a simple chairlift before?"

Chagrined that she had just been considering that very thing, Doris snapped back. "Well, we've never needed one before so why would we now?"

Donna eyed her calculatingly. "I'll tell you what. You look like a reasonable sort. Here's my counteroffer. I'll pay your ridiculous rate and you install the lift now. Surely what you'll fleece me for will pay for the damn thing."

Doris closed her eyes briefly. The clock was ticking. She had to get rid of this woman and fast.

"I'll consider it. Now if you'll excuse me." She slammed the door on her.

She could hear Donna's muffled exclamations through the heavy mahogany door, but she was beyond caring. With another muttered curse, she began to make her way laboriously up the stairs.

Lily rolled her suitcase down the hall, a battered blue Samsonite plastered with Disneyland stickers. From the other rooms came thumping and banging as the women sorted and packed their clothing and toiletries. Reaching the dumbwaiter, she hoisted it inside awkwardly.

The rumble of wheels behind her marked Betty's arrival.

"Here. Let me give you a hand with that." Lily said as she grasped the handle of Betty's leopard print rolling bag.

She gave it a tug.

It didn't budge.

"Geeze Louise! What did you pack, lady?"

"Just my things." Betty was sullen.

"It's only going to be for a couple of days you know."

"Well, I don't know what the weather is going to be like, and I am NOT re-wearing my clothing. You know, Doris sometimes forgets she's not the boss of us you know."

"I know, I know. Here, give me a hand lifting this."

With some grunting, the two women maneuvered it into the oversized dumbwaiter. Lily slid the door shut with a thud and pressed the button.

The waiter started down with its customary creaking and groaning.

"You know she cares about us, Betty."

Betty sniffed. "She thinks I'm losing my mind. There's nothing wrong with me...is there?"

Lily sighed. "Let's get downstairs. Maybe we can grab a bite before they are ready too."

Lily headed down the back stairs with Betty trailing behind her. "You know, we are all kinda worried about you lately. You just haven't seemed like yourself."

They emerged in the back hall and turned into the kitchen. On the side wall, the dumbwaiter's doors had slide open automatically. Betty sighed as they tugged on her bag. "I'm fine. I'm just having some fun, you know? Haven't you ever had fun?" They pulled the bags free and rolled them over to the back door.

"I think once back in 1982..." Lily's eyes had taken on a faraway look.

Behind them, the dumbwaiter's door slid shut as it was called for upstairs again. It began its noisy ascent to the second floor.

A moment later it came groaning down again, sliding open to reveal Rita's black American Tourister rolling bag. She clacked down the stairs behind it.

"Where's Doris?" Betty asked.

"She just started packing. That awful Donna Green came by again."

"Oh, she really not that bad you know." Lily said. "She hasn't had the easiest time of it since her husband died."

"She looks like a pauper." Rita was unconvinced.

Lily snorted. "She is far from being one, let me tell you. Come on. Let's get our bags out in the garage. Maybe we can grab a snack while we wait on Doris."

They dragged their bags in a noisy train out the back door and down the three stairs to the walkway, where they made their way to the single-car garage that stood at the end of the driveway. Pushing the bifold doors open, they could see the silhouette of Ricky Haverill in the back seat of the Buick.

Rita shuddered.

"I can't believe we are going to drive all the way to Washington DC with that man in the car!"

Betty had stopped to peer in the side window at it. "I can't tell if it's better or worse with those glasses on him."

Lily bent over next to her and looked at him for a long moment. "Well, he sure as hell doesn't look like a dead politician anymore."

Rita hesitated then stepped up next to her. She stared for a moment then gasped. "Oh, my goodness!"

"What?" they said in unison.

"He looks like that comedian, what was his name? The one with the sunglasses and the funny eye? Was always looking down?"

Lily looked baffled.

Betty brightened. "Mitch Hedberg! He looks just like Mitch Hedberg! And he's dead too!"

"So, they even look MORE alike now, right?" Lily's lip twisted wryly.

Betty clapped her hands. "He does! He looks just like him!"

Rita glanced at her drolly. "Come on you two. Let's get these in the trunk and get back inside."

Chapter Thirteen

The refrigerator cast a glow across Lily's face as Betty and Rita rattled around pulling down plates and buttering scones. She pulled out the cold cuts and cheese, then added a bunch of grapes to the mix.

They started working together in unison.

There was a noise on the back porch, then 'tap, tap, tap' on the door.

They froze looking at each other.

"What do we do now?" Betty hissed.

Tap tap tap.

Lily put her hands on her hips and scowled. "Never have I ever seen so many people showing up here in one day!" She looked at the food longingly. "And I'm hungry too!"

"For heaven's sake!" Rita threw down the dishtowel she had been wiping her hands on and stomped to the door. She flung it open.

Sandy Case stood on the back porch; her enormous handbag slung over her shoulder. Her hair was mussed, and she had a sharp look in her eyes.

"Oh crap!" Lily blurted.

Sandy gave her a wry look. "Why it's nice to see you too, Lily!" She stepped forward. Rita moved to block her way.

"Do you mind? We've had a trying couple of days, and we were just about to eat."

Sandy's eyes darted around the table and the women.

"I won't keep you long." She stepped past Rita and into the kitchen.

"Damnitall." Lily muttered.

Sandy set her bag down and slid a chair out. She smiled brightly at the sullen women. "Now why aren't you happy to see me? We've always gotten along just fine before."

"Yeah, well you hadn't barged into our house before either." Lily's jaw was set in a stubborn line. Sandy cocked her head at her. "You let Dana Oakes in. And you KNOW she's not someone you can trust."

"And you ARE?" Rita shot back at her.

Sandy settled into the kitchen chair and gestured at the food. "Don't let me keep you from your meal."

Lily reluctantly opened the bags of cold cuts and cheese. "What do you want, Sandy?"

"Oh, I was just passing by and thought it would be fun to tell you about the great visit I had with someone today."

Betty swiped a knife full of butter across a scone. "Oh? Who was that?" she answered in a distracted tone.

"Cyrus Morton."

The women froze.

Lily glanced nervously at Sandy. "So, how's old Cyrus these days?"

"A little perplexed as you might imagine. Seems he had to help you ladies out with getting rid of a rolled-up carpet Monday morning. Monday morning early, he told me. Said it was heavy as sin. He also said he thought it looked like a corpse, although he laughed when he said it."

Lily flushed and looked at the table.

In a carefully bored tone of voice, Rita replied, "Oh, yes, he was kind enough to stop and give us a hand. We were trying to get that old thing loaded up so we could take it over to the Goodwill."

Sandy fixed a laser stare at her. "Really? That's funny. They reported they never got any donations from you this week, nor did they get any carpets either."

The women cast nervous glances at each other.

"Well, that's because we took it over to Rangely to the Goodwill over there." Betty said, cool as a cucumber.

Sandy frowned at her. "Now why would you drive all the way over there when you could have just dropped it off here?"

"I had some shopping to do." Betty slapped the scone onto the plate with the others.

"You mean you don't do all your shopping here?" Sandy looked frankly dubious.

"Not when it's specialty shopping I don't."

"What's in Rangely that isn't here?"

Betty sniffed. "That Ladies Only shop on Fourth Street."

Sandy's jaw dropped. "The...Ladies Only store?"

"I just said that didn't I?"

"You mean to tell me you went shopping in a dildo store?"

Lily snorted, her face reddening. She covered her mouth with her hand. "Oh honey. If you only knew!"

This time it was Sandy's turn to blush. She looked around the table at the food and dinner plates, a frown on her face. "I know Dana was already here, and I heard that they're saying Rick Haverill is missing and that someone who looked an awful lot like you was the last person to be seen with him."

Betty sniffed. "If I were the last person to be seen with a man, do you think I'd be needing to go to a sex toy shop?"

Rita stifled a giggle. Sandy shot her a narrow look, then reluctantly stood up, pulling her bag off the back of the chair. "Oh. Well then, I'm sorry to barge in on you like this. You know how small towns are though..."

From behind them, the dumbwaiter began to whirr and clank.

Sandy looked around, faint alarm on her face. "What the heck is that?"

Rita was already trying to guide her to the door. "Nothing. Just an old house. Thanks for stopping by. Don't let us keep you."

The dumbwaiter stopped with a groan. Four pairs of eyes stared at the doors with emotions ranging from horror to suspicion.

The door slid open revealing Doris's plaid bag and her purse. From upstairs, they could hear her labored steps as she made her way down the front staircase.

Sandy's eyes narrowed and, she slid the chair back out and resettled in it.

Doris pushed the swinging door to the kitchen open and looked at Lily and Rita first. "What? What is it?" she asked.

Then her eyes swept the room and settled on Sandy, who was giving her a narrow-eyed stare with her arms folded.

"Oh fuck me!" Doris blurted.

That was something neither she nor her husband had ever said before.

Somehow it seemed to be an appropriate first time to say it.

Chapter Fourteen

"What's with the suitcase?" Sandy tapped her pen on the pad of paper in front of her.

Doris lifted her chin. "It's nothing. I'm just going to go visit my sister for a few days is all." She looked away from Sandy.

"Oh. That's nice. When were you leaving?"

Doris hitched one shoulder up in a shrug. "In the morning."

"You know, I didn't know you had a sister Doris. Where is she?"

"That's really none of your affair, young lady!"

"Don't you think it's just a little bit odd that in the past couple of days we hear about a major politician disappearing, there's the CIA and the FBI in town, and suddenly you're going away?"

"The FBI?" Rita blurted. Sandy looked at her for a long moment. "You don't seem surprised about the CIA."

Rita turned away. Lily glanced at Doris then said, "We heard about them. Like you said, this is a small town and all. And small towns are known for gossip and getting things wrong! I don't know who that feller was with the other night, but I can tell you Betty was right here!" Sort of not a lie.

Sandy frowned. "Then why were you dragging a rolled-up carpet out of here at dawn?"

Doris sniffed. "We wanted to get it over to the Goodwill right when they opened."

"Which Goodwill?" Her eyes were glittering now.

Doris opened her mouth as Lily blurted. "We just TOLD you! The one over in Rangely! So that Betty could go shopping for a new dildo!"

"Ugh!" Doris blurted. Her face reddened.

"Is that right Doris? Did she go to a dildo shop? What's the name of it?"

"How would I know that? When I go to Rangely, I go to the Mountaintop Bookstore on High Street. I don't know... or care...where Betty or anyone else went."

Sandy sat in silence for a moment her eyes raking each woman in turn. "You know, if there's anything you'd like to get off your chest, I can help you. Unlike Dana or any other reporter out there, I can give you a way out of this in return for information about the disappearance of Rick Haverill."

"We don't know anything about that." Rita sniffed. "Honestly everyone keeps asking us about him and we are as much in the dark as you are."

Sandy's eyes narrowed. She pulled her phone out and started tapping on it.

"What are you doing?" Betty asked nervously.

"Oh, nothing." She replied. "Just shooting Jim a text." She slid the phone into her bag.

Glancing back across the kitchen her eyes lit on Doris's suitcase. "So how long were you planning on going for?"

"I wasn't entirely sure. She hasn't been well, so I thought I'd stay with her until she's better."

Sandy looked around the room. "And how about you ladies? Any trips in your near future as well?"

From her bag came the ping of an incoming text. She pulled out her phone and smiled.

"Well. You'll be glad to hear I'm getting out of your hair now." She dropped her phone back into her bag. "And I know how much of a bother it is being harassed the way you have been lately, so I arranged for some help for you so that it will stop."

"You...what?" Rita gaped at her.

Smiling sweetly, Sandy replied, "I didn't want anyone else bothering you. That was Jim." She indicated her bag with her chin. "He has an officer out front; he's going to stay there overnight so that you can have your dinner in peace and get some rest."

Doris's mouth gaped open.

Sandy smiled sweetly at her. "Get some rest, ladies! Let's talk again soon, okay?"

She stood and smiled again. "Good night now!"

The kitchen door hissed shut behind her. Her footfalls clacked off the porch and faded.

They stared at each other in the suddenly airless room.

"She didn't just do that, did she?" Rita finally said.

Doris was grim. "Oh, I'm guessing she most certainly did."

"Damn!" Lily blurted. "That woman has bigger balls than most men!"

"Well, she did come here from Chicago you know." Betty said. "Does this mean we're stuck?"

"No." Doris replied grimly. "It most certainly does not."

Chapter Fifteen

The women crossed the parlor crowded together like a school of fish. Through the lace curtains they could see the rapidly fading daylight...and the unmistakable shape of a Brownville Police car parked at the curb.

Doris let the curtain fall back in place.

"Now what?" Rita asked.

"We can't drive out of here with...that...in the car with an officer out there."

"I know, I know. Give me a second." Doris pulled the curtain back again.

Lily peered through with her. "Who do you think it is?"

Doris pursed her lips. "Well. It's second shift now, so they don't have very many on it. They're not going to put one of their best officers on babysitting us."

"That woman!" Betty snorted.

Doris tapped a finger on her lips. "Lily. Go out there and say hello to him and see who it is. Ask him if he wants anything to eat or drink."

"On it!" Lily tugged the front door open and stepped out into the evening.

They watched in silence as she went down the walk and bent over into the driver's side window. A moment later, she straightened up and made her way back in.

"Who is it?" Doris hissed.

"It's that youngster, that Damien Fellows. Man, he looks like he's about thirteen."

"Good." Doris's expression had an oddly savage satisfaction to it. "Did he say he wanted anything?"

"He said he wouldn't mind a Coke if we had one."

"Oh, have I got a Coke for him." Doris muttered.

The others cast nervous looks at each other. Doris started turbo waddling toward the back of the house. "One of you get the young man a Coke." She disappeared into the bathroom.

"Sheesh." Rita murmured. "What's with HER?"

"Forty-two years of teaching sixth grade is what." Lily said as she rummaged in the refrigerator. "Do we even HAVE any Coke?"

"I think there's a diet one in there someplace." Betty answered as Doris re-entered the room, just in time to hear her.

"Good!" she said, "That's perfect!" She carried a small box in her hand.

She crossed to the cupboard and pulled a glass out, then fussed with the tea kettle for a moment, lighting the flame beneath it. Already warm, it started to heat rapidly.

"What are you doing?" Rita asked nervously.

Doris was popping pills from the box and dropping them into the glass. Taking the kettle, she poured a splash of hot water into it, dissolving the tablets.

"We don't want Damian to stay up all night, do we?"

"Well poisoning him doesn't seem like too great an idea, you know." Lily replied. "We're already up to our tatas in trouble as it is!"

"Trouble we wouldn't be in if you'd just gotten the ice!" Doris snapped.

She dumped the first inch of soda out then took the mixture and poured it in, swirling it until she was satisfied.

"There," she said, "Lily, give this soda to Damian, would you?"

Lily folded her arms. "Not until you tell me what the heck you're doing here."

Doris smiled, a smile singularly lacking in humor. "It's just some Benadryl. We don't want him suffering any unexpected allergies now do we?"

Lily gaped at her a moment then a smile blossomed across her face. "Doris Winslow, every time I think I know you I find more tricks up your sleeve." She picked up the can. "I'll be right back!"

Lily reported Damian had accepted the soda gratefully, although he confessed, he liked regular Coke better. Lily had stood chatting until he took a few swigs, making sure he would actually drink it.

Betty fussed at the curtain in the front parlor. "Do you think he's asleep yet?"

Rita patted her arm. "Come on. We're all hungry and there's nothing we can do until he's asleep so let's go eat."

They filed back into the kitchen where the food sat forgotten. Lily snapped on a light. "Well, we don't have to worry about leaving while it's light, right?"

Doris tugged her bag out of the dumbwaiter. "I can't believe Sandy Case of all people was here when I sent my bag downstairs!"

"And I can't believe what you said when you saw her!" Lily broke into a huge grin. "Holy cow; that's something I NEVER thought I'd hear YOU say!"

Doris flushed. "That was hardly my finest moment."

Betty cackled. "No, but it's one of my top ten favorite moments with you now. He, he, he!" she cackled.

"That's enough now!" Doris put the plate of scones on the table. "Let's eat."

Rita deposited the last plate into the dishwasher as Betty wiped the counter down. "It's been an hour. Do you think that's long enough?"

Doris glanced at the clock, then at Lily. "How about you go out and see if Officer Fellows needs anything else?"

Lily pushed the last chair in and set the placemats back in the stack on the shelf. "Right-o." She headed through the swinging door.

Rita looked at Doris with a worried frown. "Doris, do you think we are doing the right thing here? Once we leave, there's no turning back."

Doris shook her head. "Once we found out he was being stuffed there was no turning back. No, we have to stay strong and stay the course."

They heard the front door thud shut. A moment later Lily pushed the swinging door back open. She held the now empty soda can in her hand.

"He's snoring like a baby out there."

Doris wiped her hands. "Let's roll, ladies.

Chapter Sixteen

"I can't believe that woman!" Rita pursed her lips, glancing nervously around her. Outside, downtown Brownville rolled by its residents having retired to their homes as the night crept in and deepened.

Doris clutched the wheel grimly her mouth set in a stubborn line. "These kids all think they can put one over on me, and then they find out they can't."

In the backseat Betty leaned on the window, trying to stay as far away from the late Ricky Haverill as she could. Lily sat on the other side of him, contemplating him silently.

Rita turned to look at her. "How'd you know about that dead comic, that Mitch What's-his-face, anyway? I can't say I've ever heard of him."

Lily shrugged. "The boys on the farm loved him for some reason. I never did think he was all that funny, but they did." She eyed Ricky again for a moment. "He even wore red glasses like our friend here."

Doris shuddered. "Those eyes. What in God's name was

Hiram thinking, not only stuffing him but putting those eyes in too?"

Lily reached out and manipulated one of the arms. It flexed and bent with a faint ratcheting sound. "You gotta admit, he was right clever with it. That boy is on to something here."

Rita whipped her head around. "Don't tell me you're going to encourage him to do that again! I don't care what the state laws say: taxidermy on a human may be legal but it sure isn't right!"

"Come on now! Look at the job he did. You gotta admit he worked well under pressure. These things normally take months if not years to do. And he produced in less than 48 hours. That's something to be proud of right there."

Betty leaned further away from the corpse. "I don't care how clever he is. I don't want to be stuck back here with it. Rita, let me take the front seat."

"Oh hell no! You started this mess; you get to ride with him."

"None of this would be an issue if you had just gotten the ice, Lily." Doris's eyes were steely in the rear-view mirror. "He'd be safe and sound in the trunk, or better yet, he'd already be back in Washington D.C., and we'd be home by now."

"You know as well as I do that we would have needed a refrigerator truck for that." Lily's jaw had taken an obstinate set.

"Ladies! Please. We can't start fighting like this. We have to get as far out-of-town tonight as we can get. Rita, look at that map again and tell me where we go once we are out on 17?"

Outside the town common appeared, softly lit by the

ornate lamps installed during the town's latest upgrade. Betty sighed and pressed her head against the glass as Doris slowed to a halt at the traffic light. She stared at the common sadly. All she had wanted was to have some fun, to feel alive again. Was that so much to a..."Gah" she jumped and shrieked as an angular bony face with one bulging eye pressed up against the glass scant millimeters from her forehead.

"What? Jesus!" Rita yelled as she caught sight of the apparition. Doris slammed the gas pedal to the floor, shooting through the still red light, causing an oncoming pickup truck to brake sharply with a squeal of tires and an accompanying shouted curse.

"Oh my God, oh my God, oh my God." Betty rocked back and forth in her seat her arms wrapped tightly around herself. "What was THAT?"

Lily was twisted around looking through the rear window. "Geeze you guys. That was only One Eyed Joe."

"Oh my land." Doris rubbed her chest as a faintness swept over her. "Oh my land." she said again.

"Relax." Lily said. "it's okay. Well, except for the getting out of town without attracting any notice that is. I think that was Bud Carlisle back there in the truck. He was not impressed by that."

Doris exhaled shakily. "Well, it can't be helped now."

Rita picked the map back up off the floor and smoothed it out. "You're going to want to follow this over to Turner then take a left on 9. We can follow 9 across the state into New York. When we get to Albany, take 87 south."

"I don't like that route. Not at all." Doris's knuckles were white on the steering wheel. "There's too many people. Too many police officers. And then we have to navigate around New York City and through that horrible New Jersey! There has to be a way around it all."

Rita bit her lower lip as she studied the map. "Well," she said slowly. "I guess we could go west on I-90 and take Route 88 across the state. Once we get to Binghamton, we can keep going south until we end up in Harrisburg, Pennsylvania. That will avoid the city stuff."

"And only add hours if not days to our trip." Lily interjected. "Bud and I used to go to the auctions down in New Holland. Sometimes we would go out that way. It's definitely not city, and it's definitely not fast."

Doris glanced at her in the rearview mirror. "We can't be caught driving down the Garden State Parkway with him," she jerked her head at the corpse, "in the car. People will notice us."

"Like they haven't noticed us already?" Lily asked dryly.

Doris shot her a glare. "We're going that way. There's got to be fewer people, so it will be easier."

Chapter Seventeen

"Dispatch to car 3, come in." Jim drummed his fingers on the dash as his radio remained stubbornly silent. He thumbed the mic again. "Car 3, Damien, come in!"

Nothing.

Beside him, Sandy frowned. "Jim, why isn't he answering?"

"I don't rightly know!"

He hung the microphone up, frustrated. "Maybe he's checking on them."

"Or maybe they outsmarted him." Sandy snorted.

"They ain't like that." Jim countered. "I've known them ladies all my life. I had Miz Winslow as my sixth-grade teacher. And Lily Harris, why I went to school with her daughter. I cain't see them being sneaky."

"Well, I certainly can!" Sandy pulled her bag onto her lap and reached around, pulling the seatbelt on and fastening it.

"What are you doing?"

"You mean what are *we* doing. We're heading over there is what we are doing."

"I cain't...we cain't...we're in my squad car!"

"You do ride alongs, don't you?"

"Well yeah, from time to time."

"Then call it a ride-along. Come on; let's swing by quick and see what's happening. With any luck he just went to take a leak or something."

Jim heaved a sigh, but turned the key and spun the wheel toward The Lady's Home. Damn, but this woman could be cantankerous sometimes!

Still, he couldn't imagine his life without her now.

"They're up to something." Sandy said breaking his reverie.

He glanced at her. "But what?" He blushed at the memory of his visit with Chief Santos. "I can't imagine what else they could possibly be up to that's gonna top that industrial sized THING that Miz O'Donnell has."

Sandy glanced over at him, a small smile playing around her mouth. "I'm thinking maybe you and I need to make a field trip over to Rangely one day, do a little shopping.

"I...wha... NO!" He flushed red.

Sandy snickered as they swung onto Sycamore Street.

They could see the dark bulk of Damien's car, still sitting at the curb where they had left him hours before.

"Well, he's still here. That's something." Sandy murmured.

Jim pulled alongside the car, driver's window to driver's window. They could see the outline of Damien in the front seat.

His head was rolled back against the headrest and his mouth hung open.

"What the HELL?" Jim pushed his car door open savagely, causing it to thud off of Damien's car.

He didn't stir.

Sandy leapt out and raced around the car.

"Is he dead? What's wrong?" She asked breathlessly.

A snore reached them.

"What the..." Jim said.

Damien snored deeply, a trickle of drool coming from the corner of his mouth.

"Oh, for Pete's sake!" Sandy sputtered.

Jim leaned in the open window. "Damien. Damien."

The snoring continued.

Leaning forward, Jim placed his mouth at Damien's ear. "DAMIEN FELLOWS! YOU WAKE UP NOW!"

Damien's head snapped forward sending spittle flying onto the dash.

"Uh...wuh?" He looked around, disoriented.

"Officer, you mind telling me WHY you are sound asleep on a guard duty?" Jim's voice was flinty.

Damien looked at him, then at Sandy. His face was the picture of bewilderment.

"I...I don't know. I was wide awake. One of the ladies even brought me a Coke, so I had caffeine too." He looked around. "What time is it?"

Sandy glanced at her watch. "Almost ten o'clock."

"Ten o'clock? It was like seven thirty or eight o'clock when I had that soda." He frowned. "I don't remember anything after that. Ten o'clock?" He looked like a small child, big eyed and scared.

Jim exhaled.

"Still think they aren't capable of being sneaky Jim?" Sandy said in a sweet voice.

"Maybe they aren't. I'm gonna go see if they're there. You wait here." He headed up the walk to the front door.

"They won't. be." Sandy called after him.

Damien Fellows opened the door and slid out. "I'll give you some backup sir!" He placed his hat, which was comically oversized on him on his head and started trotting after him.

Sandy followed.

Jim reached the front porch and rapped sharply on the door.

From a neighbor's house down the street a dog started barking.

The house was silent.

He rapped again.

Damien was shuffling along the front porch, peering into the windows. "Nope, not in the parlor. They aren't in the dining room either."

Jim shot him an exasperated look. "Hey, where'd Sandy get to?"

She appeared around the corner of the house. "Right here. And you can stop knocking on the door. They're gone."

"How do you know that?" Jim asked her.

She waved around toward the back of the house. "The garage door is open, and their car is gone."

She looked at Jim with that narrow-eyed look he knew all too well. "The question is, why? And to where?"

Damien had shrunk down in his uniform, looking even smaller than usual. "They escaped under my watch?" His voice quivered.

Jim heaved a sigh and exchanged a glance with Sandy. "They didn't 'escape' son. But they did leave when you were supposed to be keeping an eye on them."

"I don't know what happened! I was wide awake! And then Miz Lily came out and asked me if I wanted anything, so I said sure, a Coke would be great. She gave me a Coke." He frowned. "It was one a' them diet ones. I never had one a' them before. Man, those things are bitter."

"Wait, it was bitter?" Sandy's voice sharpened. "They're not supposed to be."

Jim swore softly. "They done gave him something, didn't they?"

Sandy smiled demurely at him. "Looks like it. Sure glad they aren't duplicitous, huh?"

"Go ahead. Rub it in. But now we got a problem. Where the heck did they go and why?"

Sandy was shaking her head. "I don't know, but I for one don't like people sneaking away on me."

Jim looked up at the empty house with a frown on his face. "I gotta say; I don't like any of this!"

Chapter Eighteen

"Why didn't you check the gas?" Rita slapped the hood with her hand.

"Why didn't you? You were the one who was driving!" Doris balled her fists as she felt tears prickling her eyelids.

A lone car appeared and whooshed past, the taillights dwindling into specks of red fire as it climbed the long grade out of the valley.

Around them, the land drowsed. Constellations of lights below and to the left showed a far-off town. Dairy farms dotted the flank of the hill to the right, little islands of light marking the spots.

Route 88 carved a long, lonely swath here. Doris found herself wishing she had chosen the perils of New Jersey after all.

"I'm hungry." Betty wailed. "I wanted to stop for food back on the highway, but you wouldn't do it. If you had, we'd have food and fuel now."

"Someone will stop." Lily said confidently. "This is farm country. Farmers help each other out."

Rita looked around at the still night nervously. Other than the faintest whoosh of far off, unseen traffic, they were alone. Somewhere in the dark cloud of treetops below the road to the left an owl hooted mournfully. She shuddered.

From down the hillside, they heard the grumble of a large diesel motor shifting down as it prepared to haul tons of cargo up the long grade.

"Hey!" Lily said brightly. "Here comes a truck. They're Knights of the Road. He'll stop and help us."

"More like the rapists of the road." Betty wrung her hands.

Lily rolled her eyes. The motor's growl grew louder, twin beams of light swept over their car where they sat in the breakdown lane, the yellow hazard lights flashing.

Lily stepped around to the rear of the car. "Hey!" She waved her arms vigorously. "Hey! Come on, stop and give us a hand."

The truck responded by moving over one lane to allow a wider berth as it growled past with a swoosh.

"You asshole!" Lily shouted after it.

"It's just as well." Rita replied. "I agree with Betty. I'm not comfortable with some hulking truck driver anywa..."

"Hey!" Lily was staring up the hill. "Look. He's stopping."

In a pull off up the hillside the brake lights glowed as the truck halted. There was a long hiss of the air brakes and then the hazard lights began to flash on it.

"See? I told you they would help us."

Doris stared up the hill as a thousand different thoughts raced through her mind. None of them were comforting.

"Oh I don't like this. I don't like this at all!" Betty moaned.

"Will you stop? We just need someone to help us get

some gas." Lily squinted at the distant truck. "I think he just got out of it."

"We can't let him look inside the car!" Doris blurted as a cold sweat broke out on her face. Why, oh why hadn't they checked the gas when they switched drivers?

They stared in nervous silence up the hill as faint footfalls began to reach them.

"What if it's a rapist?" Rita muttered.

Lily rolled her eyes. "If YOU were a rapist, and you came upon US, would you be turned on by us?"

"You do have a point." Doris responded.

"Hey! Speak for yourself!" Betty spun around and glared at Lily. "SOME of us are still desirable you know."

The footsteps drew closer.

The women fell silent and clustered closer together. Betty reached up and took Rita's arm for comfort.

A flashlight blinked on, painting a thin strip of light on the pavement. It arced up and fell on their faces, causing them to blink in the sudden light.

"You ladies alright? What's the matter here?"

The voice belonged to a diminutive woman, barely five feet tall. Doris felt her knees go weak.

"Oh thank goodness." She blurted. "We ran out of gas, and we are in a pickle."

The woman was short and stout. Baggy jeans covered her legs down to the battered cowboy boots. She had a sleeveless plaid shirt on under a black leather vest. Her face was wizened, her hair in haphazard tufts loosely contained by a dirty red bandanna. She squinted at them suspiciously.

"The only reason I stopped was because I could see you ladies were in a jam. I don't normally stop like that." Her eyes swept around the little group. "There's too many creeps and rapists out these days."

"Thank you. Thank you so much." Doris gushed nervously. "We just need to get ahold of someplace to bring us some gas."

The woman scanned them in silence for a moment, her eyes squinting suspiciously. "Why dincha call for someone yourself?"

Doris and Rita exchanged looks. Lily stepped forward. "That's because we didn't bring a phone with us."

The woman snorted and dug a tin from her vest pocket. Eyeing them she pulled a plug of chewing tobacco out and inserted it in her cheek.

Rita shuddered at the sight.

"Well you picked a terrible place to run out and not have a phone." She finally answered. "I can call dispatch and ask them to send a tow truck out."

"Oh, we don't need a tow!" Doris said hurriedly.

"Well of course you don't." The woman replied. "They're the ones who bring the gas with them." Her expression said, 'you dummy.'

"Oh, oh yes of course. " Doris stammered. My land, but it was dark out here.

The woman looked at the small group in silence for a moment, her jaw moving as she chewed the plug of tobacco. She eyed the car. "Well, ain't that a relic? I haven't seen one of those in forever." She stepped toward it.

Doris saw black spots in front of her eyes.

Lily moved to intercept her, but the woman was already at the passenger side rear door, peering suspiciously into it.

"Hey. Who's that?" She jerked her chin at the silent black hulk that was the late Ricky Haverill.

Betty raised her chin. "That's my boyfriend, Ricky."

The woman looked over her shoulder at the group. Her gaze was not friendly. "Well why isn't Ricky here trying to help you?"

"He uh, he's had a long day." Rita said. "He's trying to catch some sleep."

"Oh yeah?" The woman stared hard at him. "Then why ain't he moving?" She reached up and rapped hard on the window. "Hey! Hey you!"

Ricky, of course, never moved being that any biological means of moving left him the moment he had his grand finale on top of Betty.

The woman straightened up and stared hard at the four of them. "So why isn't he moving? You have a corpse back there or something?"

"He's sleeping." Betty said in a weak voice.

"Then why didn't he wake up?"

"Um, because he's deaf and blind." Lily interjected.

Doris felt her knees going weak. She looked around frantically hoping for something... anything to save her from this line of inquisition, a line that was sure to land them all in a New York jail before the night was over.

"So." she said in as firm a tone as she could manage. "Are you going to call your dispatcher? We sure could use a hand getting some gas and getting out of here. We have a long way to go yet."

"Yeah? Where you headed to?" Not ready to give it up, the driver spat a thin stream of nasty fluid on the ground next to the front tire.

Doris was suddenly flummoxed. She opened her mouth, and no words came out.

Lily stepped into the breach. "We are headed to a specialty hospital in Binghamton for Ricky here. He has narcolepsy on top of his handicaps. He's also sensitive to light so we can only travel at night."

The woman eyed them with a narrow gaze. "Oh yeah? Huh. My uncle had that. Died on I-70 after falling asleep hauling a load of potato chips one night." She spat again, glanced back at Ricky, this time with less suspicion and more curiosity. "You ladies sit tight. I'll call dispatch and I'll take a break until I see the truck here." She looked around the lonely landscape. "You gotta be careful. There's always weirdos driving through here. Hell, half of them have bodies in the trunk."

"Well, I can say for a fact we don't!" Lily stated brightly.

Doris closed her eyes as the now ever-present headache bloomed again.

"Ha, well no, I guess not." The driver leaned over to take one last look at Ricky. "If this fella wakes up, he'd scare them off. He's a right big guy."

"Oh is he ever." Betty said dreamily.

Rita elbowed her sharply.

With one last stream of tobacco spittle, the woman turned and headed back up the roadway.

Her flashlight beam dwindled to a spark as she reached the black bulk of her idling rig.

Doris sagged against the car, sweat running down her temple.

"Dear God! We can't let the tow truck man see Ricky."

They stared at him silently a moment. Lily slowly said, "Well, I reckon if we unbuckle him and lay him over in the seat, he'll be less visible, right?"

"But where are we going to sit?" Rita was aghast.

"We can sit him back up when we leave you know."

"Well... I guess." Rita cast a worried look up the hill

where the truck still idled. "I did not like how interested she was in us and him."

"No." Doris agreed. "We had best keep a low profile and get out of here as fast as we can."

Another car appeared on the road, its engine whining as it pushed against gravity on the steep grade. It swooshed past without slowing.

"Not a very busy road, is it?" Betty murmured.

"No. No, it's not. I think Lily is right. Let's unbuckle him and lay him over. With any luck the driver will never see him."

Lily crossed around to the rear door and opened it. Light bloomed. She slammed the door shut. "Geeze Louise! We can't have that light on. Betty, come over here. When I open the door, you press that switch in the jamb to kill the light. Doris, Rita, I can take his upper body and will pull this way. You two get his legs up. Ready? Let's do it."

Lily opened the door again but was ready this time. She fumbled on the jamb, finding the switch and killing the light. "Okay, Betty. Put your hand right where mine is. Good. Okay ladies, come in on your side now."

They opened the other door. Doris winced as a sharp pain lanced up from her hip. Trying not to think about it too much, she grasped the pant leg firmly. Rita leaned in and grabbed onto his leg too, just above her hands. Lily braced herself from the other side. "Okay, ready? On three now...one, two..."

From down the hill came the growl of another truck motor. From up the hill, they heard the distinct slam of a door on the idling truck. A pinpoint of light bloomed as the woman began to walk back down the roadway toward them.

"THREE!"

Lily gave a tremendous pull on the upper body as Doris and Rita hauled up on his legs.

No longer carrying the weight of the live Ricky Haverill, the considerably lightened corpse flew up and over sideways before promptly sliding down into the footwell of the car.

"Shit!" Lily hissed.

Up the road, the light drew closer. Down the road the engine growl grew. As the truck came into view, they saw the distinctive flashing yellow lights on it.

"That's the tow truck." Rita said in a faint voice.

"Nothing for it now. Leave him where he is. Come on, let's close the door." Lily said.

Footsteps crunched closer as the headlights of the truck swept over them. The four women stood blinking in the light, looking to Doris's eye at least, guilty as hell.

The woman shined her flashlight across their faces. Her face puckered up into a scowl.

"What's going on here?"

Her last words were drowned by the heavy growl of the tow truck as he pulled over behind their car.

The woman looked at him then back at the four. "I'm not sure what's going on here, but I'm done. Ernie here," she jerked her head toward the truck. "He'll take it from here."

"Th.. thank you." Rita called out in a quivering voice.

"Hmph. Hope your friend gets better. Hey... where is he?"

The interior of the car was lit up from the truck parked behind it.

The back seat looked empty.

"Oh, oh, um, he had to go to the bathroom, you know?" Lily waved her hand toward the embankment.

"I thought you said he was deaf and blind?" Her voice had hardened.

"Only when he's asleep." Lily replied brightly.

The driver frowned a moment then shrugged. "Whatever. Hope he watches his step, or he's going to end up in the Schenevus Creek. Well good night and good luck to you ladies and your friend."

She looked over as the door opened on the tow truck, disgorging a man of rotund proportions. "Hey Ernie, you old skull digger. You find a job yet?" She cackled.

"Oh hush your mouth DeeDee. I work harder than you do."

She cackled again and spat a thin stream. "Make sure these ladies and their friend get underway safely now." Her eyes swept them. "Somehow I don't think they do this sort of thing very often."

"That's for sure." muttered Doris.

She turned and started back up the hill.

"Thank you!" Doris called after her.

Ernie was tugging a big can off the back of the truck. "I gotcha five gallons." He eyed the car a moment. "That usually gets people a good hundred miles or so, but I'm thinking you may want to jump off at the next exit and fill up proper." He pulled a book out of his pocket. "Now who's paying for this here fuel?"

"Here." Rita stepped forward. "I'll get it. How much is it?"

"It's $4.50 a gallon, so it's $22.50."

"WHAT? That's highway robbery!" Rita's mouth hung open.

"Hey, delivery fee. Take it or leave it."

Doris took Rita's arm. "Just do it. We'll settle up after. We don't have much choice."

Muttering, Rita yanked the door open and grabbed her purse from the front seat.

Ernie muscled the can into place and released the fuel into the tank. The sharp smell of gasoline stung their noses. He looked around as the last drops filtered in. "Where's your friend? DeeDee said you had a big guy with you."

Doris and Lily exchanged looks.

"He's, um, he's asleep in the back."

"Oh. I thought I heard you say he was taking a leak."

"No, no he's back." Lily said hastily.

Ernie was round and weathered, from years of picking up breakdowns on the highways in all seasons. There wasn't much he hadn't seen. He was silent for a moment looking at the little group then shrugged.

"Huh. Okay, well go ahead and fire her up. You should be good now."

Doris opened the driver's side door, wincing at the light. Ernie frowned.

"Hey. Where's your friend? I don't see anyone in the car."

"He, uh, he wanted to stretch his legs, so he walked on. We are supposed to pick him up after." Lily replied. Sweat was beading up on her forehead despite the cool night.

Ernie stared hard at her then looked up the stark stretch if I-88 as another vehicle, this one a lifted pickup truck roared by.

"Here? This ain't the safest place in the state to be taking a walkabout you know. And how'd he get from inside the car to outside the car like that, anyway?"

"Well, I imagine he used the door like we do." Betty said calmly. "You just didn't see him is all."

Ernie stared at her for a long moment then shook his head.

Lily glanced over the embankment toward the lights below. She gestured toward them. "He headed to that town. Told us to come pick him up once we are fueled up again. I think he was planning on taking that road down there into town."

Ernie looked over the embankment then back at them with incredulity in his face. "He...is walking down this here hillside?"

"Uh huh! He needed to get his steps in." Lily smiled brightly. "Now thank you kindly sir. We had best get going so we can go catch up with him." She grasped Rita's arm, pulling her around the car to the opposite side from the driver. "Betty, you get the front now. Rita and I will take the back."

"What?" Rita hissed at her. "I don't want to sit back there!"

Lily opened the door shoving Rita in ahead of her. "Thank you kindly sir."

Betty clambered in the front as Lily pushed her way into the back seat with Rita, their knees up to their chins as they rested their feet on Ricky.

Doris started the car with a welcome roar. "Oh, thank heavens!"

Lily waved at Ernie who stood in the same spot, with a dumbfounded look on his face.

"Doris! Get out of here!" Lily hissed as she smiled brightly at Ernie.

Doris pulled away with a jerk, leaving Ernie dwindling in the rearview mirror.

"I am... I am NOT sitting here with my feet on a dead man." Rita tried to scramble her feet up onto the seat. Lily waved out the side window at Dee Dee whose truck was still sitting in the pull-off. "Shut up Rita. It's just until we are clear of those two."

"Good lord! This just keeps going from bad to worse." Rita had managed to draw her feet up under her on the seat.

As they crested the hill, an exit sign glowed in the lights. "I'm getting off here." Doris announced. "We have to get him situated and we need to stop somewhere for fuel."

"And food." Betty announced. "I'm hungry."

As they entered the exit ramp, Doris thought to herself about how she had envisioned her life as a retired woman as quiet, predictable and neat. Nothing like this at all.

Chapter Nineteen

"Ungh." Lily exclaimed as she tugged on Ricky's very stiff, very dead arm. Grasping his sleeve, she balanced him and fished for the seatbelt that Rita was passing to her. With a click she secured him back in place in the passenger side rear seat.

"Phew." She crawled backwards across the rear seat as Rita slammed the door shut on him with a thunk. Doris leaned against the driver's door, feeling her legs shaking so hard she wondered how she was standing.

Betty stood beside her staring blankly at the scene.

Lily glanced up toward I-88, then down the dark road ahead of them. "We best be getting to that town, or we are going to be back in the same boat."

She looked at Doris for a moment. "I'll drive. Come on, take a break Doris."

Betty started toward the passenger side, but Rita took her arm firmly. "No. You ride in back for now. Let Doris relax."

Betty's lower lip jutted out dangerously. "But I can't ride in the back! I get car sick."

"Oh for Pete's sake Betty!" Rita gave her arm a tug. "Come on, let's go. We need to find a gas station."

Betty pulled her arm away and huffed. For a moment she looked like she was going to stand her ground, but instead her shoulders slumped and she came around to the rear of the car. She stopped again. "I can't ride next to him!" she wailed.

"Well why not? You were more than happy to ride ON him." Lily snapped.

Rita rolled her eyes. "Fine. I'll take the middle then. Just get in so we can get going."

"Can we go eat?" Betty asked as she buckled in.

Lily glanced at Doris. "You know, I think that's a good idea. We can fuel up, eat, take a break and figure out where we are going tonight."

Doris simply nodded. Lily eyed her with concern. "I think some food will do you good." she said to her.

The Gas 'N Go glowed red and white on the roadside as they drew near. They pulled in, the only customers Rita was glad to note. The tiny convenience store window sported a long crack from corner to corner, held in place by energy drink and beer posters. The pumps were rusty with loose panels that creaked slightly in the night breeze. Inside a lone man stared out at them avidly.

Doris shuddered.

"Let's get our gas and get out pronto." She muttered to Lily. "I'm not liking this place at all."

"Got it."

Lily crossed around to the pump and inserted her credit card, then pulled the pump and slid it into the Buick's fuel filler. She was glad Ricky was on the other side: he was giving her the creeps and she wasn't certain, but she thought he may have been starting to smell just a tiny bit. She pushed the thought away.

"Evening." The deep baritone behind her made her jump.

The man had come out of the station and was standing some eighteen inches away from Lily. He wore denim overalls which barely contained a large midsection. Up close, he sported holes where teeth had once been and a balding head with a bad comb over. His face was stubbled with a heavy unibrow. He leered at Lily.

"Can I help you with that?"

Her heart was pounding in her throat. Lily sidled around so she was facing him, the pump working maddeningly slow.

"I think we can handle it." she replied in a cool tone.

He eyed her a moment then leaned over to look in the car. His eyes raked the women, stopping on Betty.

"So where are you ladies heading to tonight? We don't get many visitors here."

"Just passing through." Lily was curt.

"Who's that lovely lady in the back here? She looks like a movie star." He smiled at Betty, a grotesque parody of one that somehow made him even more unattractive.

Betty, for once, stared at him coldly.

He straightened up and waddled around the car, stopping at the passenger side rear. He bent over as Doris gasped and flung her door open.

"And who is... whoa, hey now!" He jumped back visibly startled at the sudden appearance of Ricky's moon white face and red sunglasses.

Doris drew herself up in her best sixth-grade teacher stance. "We don't need your help, thank you."

He stared at her then back at Ricky. "Who's yer friend?" He jerked his chin at him.

"That's none of your business."

Lily finished pumping and tugged the nozzle out, spraying droplets everywhere in her haste. The night pressed in around them, dark and humming with insects, bringing home just how isolated they were. She eyed the station man narrowly. She wasn't sure, but it looked like he had the bulge of a pistol under his overalls. He and Doris were in a silent standoff, glaring at each other, Betty and Rita white faced in the back seat.

She didn't like this, not at all.

She twirled the cap on the fuel filler and closed the door. "Come on Doris. We are all done here."

"Whoa now, who said you are all set?" The man's face had taken on a dark, calculating look. "Maybe I want to get to know this fine lady here." He looked in the window at Betty again, scowling as he saw Ricky's moon white face. "What's wrong with this here fella? Why's he wearing sunglasses at night? You aren't engaged in some sort of crime, are you?"

Doris blanched, visible in the flickering sodium light.

Lily stared at him a long moment her face hard. "We aren't but we are about to be." She said.

"Huh?" He stared at her baffled.

She pulled the nozzle out again and flipped the lever. The pump rattled back to life. She aimed the nozzle at him. "You have two seconds to get back inside before you get a gasoline bath." Her voice was cold. "And don't even think of reaching for your piece or you're going to find out how fast I can light a match."

His jaw gaped. "Now, whoa, whoa...I was only tryin' to..."

"One second left, sir." She held the nozzle aimed at his face in a hand that was steady.

He raised his hands and backed away. "Okay, okay already. Damn you ladies are suspicious. I was tryin' to make nice here."

"Time's up."

"Jesus!" He whirled and shuffled away quickly glancing at them over his shoulder with a dark glare. "I'm going already. But I'ma gonna remember you!"

"Good. Let's hope you do the next time you try to harass a woman."

She glanced at Doris. "Get in now!" she hissed.

Once Doris was safely in the car, she replaced the nozzle and jumped into the driver's seat. The tires chirped as she sped out of the lot.

"Oh my land!" Doris held her chest with one hand and the door with the other. Lily sped down the roadway glancing at the rear-view mirror. When they were far enough away, she slowed and fished around for her seatbelt.

"Oh my God." Rita exclaimed. Betty sat mutely her face drawn in fear. Lily glanced at her in the rearview mirror.

"Maybe being where there aren't a lot of people isn't a good idea after all."

"Well, it's too late now." Rita replied. "Where do we go now? If we go back to the highway, we have to pass that terrible place again."

"I know, I know. I'm going to go this way for a bit and find a place where we can stop and look at the map."

"Is that light ahead?" Doris sat up, peering through the windshield.

Ahead of them, streetlights bloomed.

"A town!" Betty cried.

Lily exhaled. "Okay. Okay then. Let's see what we have and find someplace to stop."

Dark woodlands began to give way to houses and lawns, then a church and fire station. The lights grew brighter as they approached what appeared to be a town center.

"Look!" Betty pointed, "There's a restaurant!"

It wasn't much of one, but it was a bar and grill. The one-story building was covered in brown clapboarding. Overgrown flower-pots bracketed the front door. Red and blue neon lights advertising beer brands and an 'open' sign glowed. The parking lot held six cars.

"We have to stop here. We need food." Rita said.

Lily and Doris exchanged looks. "I don't know, I'm not real comfortable about this." Doris said.

"It probably won't take long." Lily told her. "Grab a few burgers and get out. We can check the map and find the best way back to the highway that doesn't involve going by that wretched man."

"What about our friend here?" Rita looked askance at Ricky.

Lily glanced over the back of the seat. "It's dark, and if we are fast about it we can get in and out with no one nosing around him."

"I still don't like this." Doris muttered.

"We don't have many options, Doris." Lily's jaw was set. "No, let's do this and get going again. We still have to find a place to stay tonight too."

She swung into the parking lot.

Chapter Twenty

The car doors thumped hollowly as the women shut them. Betty yawned and stretched, shifting her oversized purse from one shoulder to the other. They stared at the front of the bar and grill with emotions ranging from hopeful to mistrustful. A faded blue and red sign swung in the breeze on a pole at the edge of the parking lot, the name 'Do Drop In' in weathered cursive writing. A neon sign advertising a beer brand flickered unevenly in the front window.

Doris frowned. This was not her kind of place, no sir, not at all. She looked around at the others. "Let's make this fast, ladies."

They headed toward the entrance in a fast shuffle.

Lily glanced over her shoulder at the car. "Think we should get Ricky something?" She chuckled.

Rita looked at her aghast. "How can you make jokes about something like that?"

"Oh, come on now. You gotta admit, in some ways it's turning into a comedy. Did any of you think we would be taking a trip like this?"

Doris shuddered. "Lord no! And I can't say I want to be making this one!"

Betty glanced back at the car, a vaguely wistful look on her face. "I would have loved to have gone on the campaign trail with Ricky. I know what it's like to be a politician's wife."

"And now you know what it's like to be his mistress too." Rita muttered.

"Ladies! Enough!" Doris reached for the door handle. "Focus. We get in and out. Then we find a place to stay tonight."

She tugged the heavy wooden door open.

Tinny music from a jukebox greeted them, Tammy singing about standing by her man.

A tired overweight blonde woman was wiping the bar down. Six sets of eyes were cast on them from the patrons scattered around the dimly lit room.

The blonde didn't bother looking.

Three men sat at the bar, various glasses in front of them. An older couple sat at one of the tiny tables in the dining area, and a single man in a neon construction vest sat methodically devouring a plate of fries and a burger at another.

Over along the side wall, the waitress sat perusing the help wanted ads. She glanced up at them and frowned slightly, then rose to greet them.

Lily looked around the room openly as Doris eyed Betty out of the corner of her eye.

One of the men at the bar was staring at her.

"Four?" The waitress had brunette hair haphazardly piled on her head and a black apron at her waist. A pencil was stuck above her left ear.

Rita nodded primly, clutching her purse in front of her. "Yes, four please."

She led them to a larger table in the back center of the room, took drink orders and left them.

The couple had stopped eating and was staring at them.

"Why is everyone looking at us?" Betty wanted to know.

"It's small-town syndrome." Lily replied. "If you see the same people over and over, someone new is reason to stare."

"They don't do this in Brownville." Betty said.

"Brownville is a lot bigger than this town."

Betty looked around the room. "So where are we, anyway?"

The waitress had returned as she said it, carrying four waters, two teas and one coffee.

"What, you don't know where you are?" She laughed as she said it.

"We had a breakdown on the interstate so we got off to get some food and fuel." Doris replied stiffly.

"Oh. Well welcome to beautiful Quarry Town, New York, population 848 on a good day." She plunked the drinks town on the table.

"Only 848 people?" Lily said. "It looks like this is a larger town than that."

"It was once. We had the mill and the quarry. In the daylight you can see the houses from the mill era, all along the side streets. But that closed in the 1960s. We still had the quarry, they used to mine titanium there. Made a mighty good living for a while too. But that ran out in the 1980s. They closed it for good in '89 or so." She shrugged. "The companies left and most of the people left with them."

"That's so sad." Rita said. "To have your town just up and die like that."

"So, what to people do for a living here now?" Lily asked.

"Mostly farming and meth labs."

"Whu...what?" Lily's eyes were round.

"Wish I was lying but I ain't."

Doris glanced around the table. "I think we are going to take this to go please."

"Suit yourself." She took their orders then shuffled off to the kitchen.

They fell into an uneasy silence. On the jukebox, Tammy gave way to Waylon who gave it up to Dolly. The other patrons went back to their meals and ignored them.

Rita glanced at the bar and leaned forward. "That man on the end, he hasn't stopped staring at us since we walked in."

Doris pursed her lips. "Ignore him. Let's get our food and leave as soon as we can."

Betty was staring at the bar. "I think he's looking at me! He likes me!"

Lily rolled her eyes. "We look at you too, but it doesn't always mean we like you."

"Hey!" Betty's head whipped around her expression stricken.

"Lily, would you stop that? Betty, she didn't mean it. Did you Lily?" Doris pinned her with her best sixth-grade teacher stare. Lily shifted uncomfortably. "Ah come on Betty you know I'm pulling your leg."

Over at the bar, the man put his glass down and tossed a bill on the counter. With one last look at the women, he headed out the door.

"Phew." Rita muttered. "He gave me the willies."

Betty's lower lip stuck out petulantly. "I still say he liked me."

Doris closed her eyes briefly as the headache throbbed again. She wondered if her blood pressure was acting up again. When this...escapade was over, she was going to call Dr. Murphy's office and make an appointment for a checkup.

If they made it out okay that is.

They fell into an uneasy silence as they waited for the food. The jukebox whirred and hummed, as one ballad replaced another.

Finally, the tired brunette appeared carrying a large bag of food. "Here ya go. Sorry. Kitchen had kind of an emergency."

"Oh. I hope everything is okay." Rita had opened the bag and was taking inventory of the contents.

"It's fine. Chef lost his glasses is all. But he found 'em again. They were in the clam chowder this time." She turned and headed back to her help wanted ads.

Doris's face contracted. She looked around the table. "Did anyone order the soup?"

"No, no soup." Rita started replacing all the items in the bag. "Let's go."

Doris inhaled the night air gratefully as they exited the bar. "My land! I can't believe this place has managed to stay in business!"

"Well, they sell alcohol. I think the food is an afterthought." Lily said.

"I'm hungry. Let's eat now!" Betty reached for the bag. "I ordered French fries. Where are they?"

"Hang on. Let's get the car and go someplace to eat." Rita replied.

They rounded the corner of the bar.

"What the...? HEY!" Lily shouted.

The interior light was on in the Buick. The reason it was on was because the back door was open.

And the back seat was empty.

"WHERE THE HELL IS RICKY?" Rita yelled.

"Oh, my land!" Doris grasped her chest as spots danced in front of her eyes. "Oh my God!"

"Ricky!" Betty was pointing across the parking lot. "Ricky!"

In the dim glow of the streetlights, they could see the man who had been staring at them in the bar wrestling with a large object he was trying to hoist into the bed of a battered pickup truck.

That large object was wearing red sunglasses.

"Oh no you don't!" Lily muttered grimly. She took off in a dead run, with Betty right at her heels. Doris and Rita followed. Doris winced as the pain tore through her hips.

"Hey! You! What do you think you're doing?" Lily shouted. She gave him a hard shove sending his staggering sideways. He lost his grip in Ricky who fell to the ground still in his seated position. Rita dove in and grabbed Ricky, sliding her arms under him from behind and lifting him in a full Nelson. The man scrambled to his feet and grabbed her by the hair, giving her a savage yank. Rita yelped in pain as she lost her grip on Ricky and fell backwards.

Lily leapt forward and drew her right leg back. She let loose with a roundhouse kick that connected solidly with his kneecap. He yelled in pain and released Rita, whirling toward Lily with a fist cocked. He swung at her, missing as she ducked. With a muttered curse, he lashed out and grabbed her by her shoulder, drawing her in, his fist drawn back ready to clobber her. She threw her arm up to deflect it as Betty ran up to his side. Her arm flashed and there was a squishy thud.

The man crumpled to the ground and stayed there.

"What the hell just happened?" Rita blurted, clutching the side of her throbbing head.

They looked down the now unconscious man, bewildered.

"Betty, how did you do that?" Doris looked up at her.

Betty was staring at him, a hard expression on her face. In her right hand she held Frankie.

"If I broke Frankie on this lunkhead, I'm going to hit him again."

"You...you hit him with a DILDO?" Lily put her hand over her mouth. "Oh, holy shit! You literally just cold-cocked him!"

"You brought that...thing with you?" Rita stared slack jawed.

"Well, I for one am glad she did!" Lily replied.

"We have to get out of here! Quick! Before he comes to!" Doris was starting to panic.

"I'll get the car." Lily turned and sprinted back toward it.

"He's going to tell people!" Doris felt her throat starting to close.

"Tell them what? That he broke into a car and was stealing a dead man when he was knocked out by a sex toy?" Betty stared coldly at him. "I have half a mind to hit him again for good measure.

Lily swung the Buick around in a cloud of dust. She jumped out. "Come on! Hurry up!"

She, Rita and Betty wrestled Ricky into the back seat unceremoniously. Doris clambered into the front passenger seat. They slammed the doors and roared across the lot.

"Hey!" Betty shouted. "The food!" She pointed at the bag, lying on its side forgotten. Lily swung the car next to it and opened the door. She snatched the bag off the ground without stopping.

With a squeal of tires, they hit pavement and sped away.

Chapter Twenty-One

"This door just doesn't shut right now. That jerk screwed it up." Rita fussed with the back door on the driver's side. Ricky was sprawled in the footwell again; Rita and Betty were riding with their feet propped up on him. Empty food containers peppered the seat between them.

Funny how things like resting your feet on a corpse stopped bothering you after a while, Doris thought.

Outside, the dark countryside flashed past as Lily sped down Interstate 88. A sign that read 'Binghamton 17 miles' glowed green in the headlights.

"We need to find a place to stop for the night." Rita leaned forward. "It's almost midnight."

"What are we going to do with him?" Lily asked. "We surely can't leave him in the car alone."

"Maybe we can stop and get him into the trunk." Doris replied.

"Ugh." Betty shuddered.

A highway sign advertising services at the next exit loomed, a bright blue blaze in the Buick's lights.

"Hey." Lily said, "There's a motel at this exit."

"Shouldn't we just go on to Binghamton? There's more hotels there." Rita looked dubious.

"And more people too." Lily told her. "The whole point of this route was to stay away from people."

"We really should stop." Betty said. "We are all tired."

"I agree with Betty." Doris said. "But let's take a look at the place first. If it looks bad, we move along."

Lily put the turn signal on and guided the lumbering Buick down the exit ramp. A gas station and convenience store were on the left side of the road. Further along they could see the red glow of the neon sign advertising the Windmill Motel.

"Okay, drive past it slowly." Doris said. "And take a sharp look at it to see if there's anything suspicious about it. After Quarry Town, I'm not comfortable with these small towns."

Lily craned at the motel, a single-story long building. About five cars dotted the lot, a plastic lawn chair was outside each room. The sign advertised 'Pool, Wireless Internet'

There was a light on in the office. They could see a woman sitting at the desk.

"Well?" Lily asked as the motel slid into their rearview mirror.

"Let's try it." Rita said.

Doris nodded.

Lily made a U-turn and headed back to it.

A bell tinkled merrily as Doris and Rita entered the brightly lit office. Behind the counter, a red-haired woman looked over her glasses at them as they entered. The walls were covered with posters of local attractions; a brochure stand filled the wall next to the door.

"Evening ladies. You checking in?"

Doris stepped up and opened her purse. "We need a room please, one with two beds."

Rita looked around the small room. Her eye fell on the luggage cart that was parked in the foyer.

"We need to use this." She said.

The woman didn't glance up as she took Doris's information. "Help yourself."

Ten minutes later, Doris walked out and returned to the car. Rita was already there with the cart. Luggage was piled high on it. She looked at the empty back seat. "Where's Ricky?"

Lily waved her hand at the cart.

"Wait...what?" Doris looked at the massive jumble of luggage, confused.

"We can't leave him outside." Rita said. "Especially now that the back door doesn't work like it should."

"He's...in the luggage?"

Lily and Rita grabbed the handles and started pushing it to the sidewalk. "What's our room number?" Lily asked.

Doris stopped. "I can't...we can't...we can't possibly sleep with that...thing in the room with us!"

"I think we will sleep better than we would if we had to worry about him all night." Lily stopped in front of the door. "Gimme the key."

She pushed the door open, and they wrestled the loaded cart in.

"Phew. What a day!" Betty said as they shut the door.

The room was small but clean. They tugged their bags off the cart, revealing Ricky lying supine on the floor of it.

Doris shuddered.

Lily dragged the cover off of the nearest bed and tossed it over him. "Here. Now we don't have to look at him."

"Ugh. Put him over there!" Doris pointed at the space between the small desk and the window.

Exhausted, the women donned night clothing, did their nightly routines and fell into bed. Doris and Rita shared one Queen bed, Lily and Betty the other.

With the lights off, strange shadows painted the ceiling.

"How's your head?" Doris asked Rita.

"It hurts, but it will be alright." She replied.

Lily nudged Betty. "Nice job with Frankie out there."

"Oh please!" Doris said. "Can we not talk about that THING?"

Lily chuckled. "Come on now. I thought he was going to drill me when Betty did that. You know, Frankie has saved us a couple of times now."

"I told you Frankie was a good companion!" Betty said cheerfully.

"Heavens!" Rita exclaimed. "If he had been a better companion, we might not be in this predicament now, would we?"

They fell silent at that. A few moments later soft snores began to fill the room.

It had been one hell of a day.

Despite their exhaustion, anxiety drove them out of sleep by sunrise.

Lily peered out the curtain into the parking lot as they sleepily changed into clean clothing and freshened up.

They piled the luggage on Ricky again. Carefully, they opened the door and looked around the lot.

"Coast is clear. Let's go." Lily said.

The cart rumbled and jolted to the car. Once there, they opened the rear doors and the trunk. As quickly as they could they heaved their luggage into the spacious trunk.

Rita opened the rear door, and Ricky was wheeled over and shoved into the back seat in the middle, where Betty belted him in.

There was a thump from the trunk.

Straightening up, Rita, Betty and Doris looked at the back of the car, where Lily was wrestling the cart into the massive space along with the luggage.

"What are you doing?" Doris hissed.

"You gotta admit; he's a LOT easier to move using this. We're taking it."

"But that's stealing!" Doris told her.

"Yeah, well I think that," Lily jerked her chin at Ricky, "Is breaking laws a whole lot more serious."

"She has a point, Doris. Ricky will be a lot easier to move around this way." Rita rubbed her chin contemplatively. "I say we take it."

"Sure, it's not YOUR credit card that's going to get charged for it!" Doris felt faint as it hit her. Credit cards! They were leaving a trail behind them!

"We should be in D.C. by tomorrow night if things go okay. If we can get him into his hotel, we can just leave him there. Bring the cart back here and drop it in the parking lot." Lily slammed the trunk shut.

"You mean like how well things have been going so far?" Doris replied acidly.

Lily sighed and opened the car door.

"Time's a-wasting. Let's go."

Chapter Twenty-Two

Jim pulled into the station as the first rays of the sun were creeping up the far hill. His head ached from lack of sleep. After leaving Sandy last night, he had searched the various databases he had, trying to decipher if there was any possible explanation for their abrupt disappearance. Maybe a family member nearby they could have gone to, or an impending financial crisis looming.

Nothing.

They seemed to lead singularly boring lives.

He noticed a black Ford Explorer parked on the other side of the lot, closest to the station door. Chief Tony Santos's car was parked next to it.

The Explorer had government plates.

Jim felt his mouth go dry. He had to admit, he hadn't placed any stock in the rumor going around that Betty O'Donnell was the last person seen with the apparently now missing Vice-Presidential candidate, Richard Haverill. He knew Miz O'Donnell was a bit...odd these days, but a missing politician?

He shook his head firmly as he strode up the walk to the station. None of those ladies could do anything like that. He'd stake his career on it.

An hour later, he had to wonder if he was going to end up eating his own words.

He had left...escaped actually...leaving Chief Santos and two disagreeable Feds arguing in his office.

He hadn't like them on sight. Harold Noth was skinny and tall, with a sloping forehead and chin. His partner, Curtis Danville was shorter and stout, with black hair and swarthy skin.

They both lacked anything resembling a personality.

Chief Santos wasn't backing down. Now maybe those ladies were up to something or maybe they weren't but either way, no one in the Brownville Police Department was going to be overly helpful to those two.

Still, when Noth slapped a grainy photograph on the desk of their missing Vice-Presidential candidate, he had to admit; the woman he was with looked an awful lot like Miz O'Donnell.

Jim had sidled over, getting a good look at the photo. He recognized the building it was from, a local credit union. His cousin Melvin was in charge of security for them.

Once he was safely in his car, away from prying eyes, he first called Melvin and asked him to send him that photo. Then he called Sandy.

"Do you never sleep?" she greeted him blearily.

"This thing's getting big." He told her.

"Why? What's happening?" her voice had sharpened drastically.

He filled her in on the two feds and the questions they were asking. Then he told her about the photograph.

"Hot damn." She breathed.

"Now don't you be going and running around for the paper about this!"

"Jim, there's a major politician missing, and he may have ended up in Brownville...what do you THINK I was going to do?"

"I was kinda hopin' that you might help me." He replied plaintively.

She was silent for a moment.

"Ah darn it all Jim."

"I know these women, Sandy. They're like family to me and lots of other folk here. If they're missing, something is wrong. They might be in trouble. Look." He sighed and rubbed his eyes. "If it turns out they're in trouble, I'd hate to splash them all over the news."

Sandy exhaled then said. "Okay. Okay. I'll help you figure it out. BUT...if it turns out they WERE up to something, then I get the exclusive and I get to print it, okay?"

Jim sat for a moment. He really didn't think they were up to anything, but he did think they might be in trouble. "Okay. Fair enough. What are you gonna do?"

"I'm going to make a phone call. I'll call you later."

She hung up.

Chapter Twenty-Three

Rita unfolded the map then refolded it to show their location. She traced a finger down it.

"Here. We take 81 once we reach Binghamton, follow it to Scranton and then Harrisburg." She glanced over at the dashboard. "How are we doing on gas? I don't want to go through a night like last night again!"

Doris glanced down at the gauge. "We have a quarter of a tank left. We should probably fill up before we leave Binghamton."

Lily looked at Ricky, who was strapped in the middle between them. In the early morning glare of the sun, the sunglasses didn't look out of place. He was a big drink of water, she thought, noticing how close to the car's roof he came.

"Think it's safe to stop with Ricky sitting up like that?" Rita had turned around in the front seat to peer worriedly at him. "It seems like he gets attention wherever we are."

"Those weird glasses might have something to do with it." Betty replied. "Maybe he's look better without them." She reached up and tugged the glasses off.

Doris glanced in the rear-view mirror at him. "Ugh! NO! That's not better, not even a little bit." She shuddered.

Lily was looking intently at his face. "You know, I hadn't really taken a moment to truly look at him without the glasses. Those eyes are just..."

"Weird." Rita finished for her. "And creepy! What was Hiram thinking putting bear eyes in him?"

"What was Hiram thinking when he agreed to gut and stuff him?" Doris's jaw had a hard set to it. "I simply cannot believe this has happened."

"We could have called the police in the first place, you know." Rita folded the map in half. "I still don't know why you wouldn't let us do that!"

Doris was silent for a moment. "I simply couldn't have all those men tromping around in our house, our life. I couldn't tolerate the things they would say about us in the newspaper." She looked in the rearview mirror again, at Betty this time. "I was not going to tolerate the things they might say about Betty."

"What would they say about me?" Betty leaned forward puzzlement evident on her face. "I didn't do anything wrong."

"Except for having the leading contender for the Vice President of the United States die in your bed, the MARRIED leading contender, I might add." Lily pointed out acerbically.

Betty looked at Ricky then back at Lily. "He, what?"

She looked bewildered.

Lily's shoulders slumped. She stared at Betty a moment, her face showing a sudden sadness.

Doris looked in the mirror again. "This is why we couldn't call the police."

They fell silent at the highway thumped under the wheels of the Buick. A sign for a gas station loomed over the treetops ahead of them. Doris put on her signal and eased off the exit.

The station was large and busy. Doris pulled into the pump furthest from the building, warily eyeing the people filling their cars. Her hips screamed in protest as she clambered out of the car.

Rita, Lily, and Betty followed suit.

Lily rubbed her back and stretched backwards, grimacing. "Why don't you and Betty go in and use the restroom first?" she said to Rita. "When you two are done, Doris and I will go."

She watched the two women as they made their way across the busy lot.

"Doris, what are we going to do about Betty? She's getting worse."

Doris heaved a shaky sigh. "I know. I kept thinking we needed to have a talk before all of...this...happened, but I kept putting it off. She would seem better, and I'd think oh, maybe she just had a bad day. Then she would get worse again. We have to do something."

"But what?" Lily leaned back against the car and folded her arms. "She doesn't have any family. And she barely has any money. She's living from Social Security check to Social Security check. What's going to happen to her? She's going to need care, more care than we can give her."

Doris felt sudden tears prick her eyes. "We will just have to figure something out. She's family. She's just an old lady trying to make her way in the world as best she can, just like us. We can't abandon her."

Lily shook her head. "No. No we can't." She looked at

Doris. "And now I understand why you reacted the way you did the other night."

Doris set her jaw. "We are family. And family takes care of family." The pump stopped, and she tugged the nozzle back out. She grimaced at the amount on the screen. "This trip is going to break me though. My land, gas is expensive!"

Lily sighed. "I know. We'll all chip in. This shouldn't be all on you." She looked across the lot. "Here they come. Let's go inside and use the restroom."

Once Rita and Betty reached the Buick, Doris and Lily made their way laboriously across the lot, well laboriously for Doris at least. Lily slowed her pace to stay at her side.

The Circle K was bustling, with crowds around the coffee and pastry area. Lily eyed it as they entered. "Why don't you go first." She said to Doris. "I'm going to get coffee and something to eat. You want anything?"

Doris waved her hand vaguely at the station. "I guess a tea and maybe a scone if they have them." She trudged toward the bathroom.

Lily grabbed cups and started perusing the selection at the air pots of coffee dotting the counter. She filled one cup, then located tea and hot water. Across the coffee island, two high school-age boys were making choices of junk food amidst much shoving and loud exclamations.

She was eyeing the selection of wrapped pastries with ill-concealed disappointment when a blonde-haired boy burst through the glass doors.

"Dude! Dude!" he hissed. "Come out here, quick! You gotta see this!"

Lily ignored him, poking through the pastries wondering what Doris might eat in place of a scone.

"What? Hey Max, lookit that! Tittie twist!" The skinny red head grabbed the brown-haired boy's chest and twisted.

"Ow! You loser!" There was a sharp smack as he punched him in the shoulder.

"Guys! Guys! You gotta see this! This dude is the dead ringer for Mitch Hedburg! Right down to the glasses!"

"What? Where? He's like dead, man, he's been unalive for years now."

"I know! It's crazy! Come on! You gotta see this! He's in that ancient car over there!"

"No shit! Look at that thing! That's like a relic!"

"No way! Ha ha ha! That's wild! Come on!"

Lily had frozen a honey bun clenched in her hand. Her mouth went dry.

Doris appeared to her right, shuffling slowly.

The boys turned and moved with astonishing speed toward the door.

Lily dropped the tray of drinks and the honey bun. She grabbed Doris's arm. "COME ON!"

She dragged Doris across the store and out the door.

The boys with their youth and long legs had already reached the pump where Rita and Betty waited. Lily could see the look of alarm on Rita's face, and an odd look on Betty's. She stared at the boys hard as they approached.

"What's going on?" Doris was turbo waddling as fast as she could.

"They spotted Ricky." Lily said grimly.

"Oh no! Why won't anyone leave us alone? Why do they all have to be all over him like that?"

"Hey!" the blonde called out to them. "Who's your friend? Is that Mitch Hedburg's son or something?"

Lily could see Rita mouth "Oh crap." when she heard that. Doris groaned. "Oh no. No, no no!"

Rita tried to block the boys, who spread around the car peering in the window.

"Oh my god! That totally looks like him! Ha ha ha! Hey mister!" the brown-haired boy rapped on the window sharply. "Hey! Mister!"

"You leave him alone!" Doris barked. "Where are your manners?"

"Is he like dead or something?" The red-head shaded his eyes, his face furrowed.

"He's asleep." Betty had stepped forward. She looked them up and down. "And who raised you? How dare you harass strangers like that!"

"Lighten up, lady. I wanna see Mitch!" He pressed his face to the glass. "Hey, how come he isn't moving? What's wrong with him?"

Betty stepped forward and pushed her way between him and the car. "Don't you make me call Frankie on you!" She clutched her bag, a grim look on her face.

Doris's jaw dropped. Oh no.

"Oooo! Who's Frankie? Some kind of a hard ass?" The brown-haired boy smirked.

"You might say that. If you're into that sort of thing." There wasn't a trace of amusement in Betty's face as she said it.

"Then let's see him. Is that Frankie?" he jerked his head at Ricky.

Betty reached into her purse. Lily slapped her hand on top of hers. "Betty! No! Don't whip it out!"

The blonde had backed up, his eyes wide. "Oh shit! Guys! Guys! She's got a gun!"

"Oh shit!" The red-head and the brown-haired boy stumbled into each other; their faces horrified.

Doris had to admit; the look on Betty's face was scaring her too.

The boys stumbled and crashed into each other in their sudden haste to get away.

Lily exhaled shakily. "Come on! Let's get out of here!"

They tumbled into the car and sped out of the lot.

Chapter Twenty-Four

"You're going to owe me for this one, Case." Jorge Maxim's voice was vaguely smug as he listened to her story.

"Yeah, well if it turns out they were up to something, YOU'RE going to owe ME."

She had hesitated at calling Jorge for a while as she turned over the pros and cons of bringing him in on this with her. Jorge had been Sandy's coworker when she first came to town. Together they had worked on a story that ended up having a national news impact, landing Jorge a Pulitzer in the process.

Riding on the success of that, he had taken a job with a major news company in Washington DC. Sandy didn't know anyone else more intelligent and more in tune with national politics than Jorge.

And he had just given her more...a lot more...background and insight on Richard Haverill's apparent disappearance. It was causing a maelstrom of uncertainty in the Capitol of the United States.

So much so that Jorge had immediately offered to fly to

Brownville to help her. He told her he would be at Hopefield, the regional airport some ten miles outside of town, in three hours.

"Wait, what? How can you do that so fast?" she had gasped.

"Because my publisher has deep pockets, and it's no holds barred on this story." He'd replied.

She squirmed inside a little, wondering how Jim would take this development. She could understand him liking someone, but news was news, and this was starting to look, smell and taste like a big story.

And she had to admit; it would be nice to see Jorge again.

Jorge was a trim Black man who always looked like he had just stepped out of the pages of a fancy men's magazine. Some 5 feet 10 inches tall, he sported close cropped hair and a thin mustache. Gold-framed glasses covered eyes that were keen and sharp. He missed nothing.

She smiled when she thought of some of the things he had gone through with her when they worked a murder case together, the one that launched his career. He wasn't always neat, clean, and unflappable.

She wondered how life in Washington D.C. was treating him.

She poked around on her computer for a while, checking various news sources for any updates on the disappearance of Richard Haverill. There were a lot of articles, but nothing that gave any new information.

Sighing she closed the lid on her laptop and slid it into her bag. Time to get outside and get some fresh air, let her brain work.

Clattering down the granite steps of the Brownville Reporter, she paused a moment then turned right, heading up Main Street. The day was warm and bright, hardly any clouds marring the sky. She started walking briskly.

She paused on the sidewalk outside of the Brownville Emporium. She let her eyes scan the downtown slowly, the tired buildings with an eclectic assortment of shops, the gently worn mountains looming over the town...and the tall bean pole of a man who was making his way up the sidewalk across from her.

One Eyed Joe was an interesting character. He was one of the homeless, or 'unhoused' as they were referred to now, who was the unofficial leader, the 'mayor' of their rag tag encampment down by the Mill River. Joe had been instrumental in helping Sandy on the murder case, and other smaller ones since then.

She changed direction and walked over to him.

He raised his brow...he had one eye, the other gone from a long-ago accident, and nodded to her.

"Hi Joe. Can I buy you a pastry?" she nodded toward the Emporium.

He nodded and smiled slightly. He knew what she wanted.

They strolled back to the iron tables in front of the Emporium. She looked at him questioningly.

"Hsinad esaelp. Yrrehc." He said.

Joe had speech dysmorphia, a rather rare condition that caused him to talk 'backwards.' Sandy had learned how to decipher his words by now.

And to hedge her bets, she carried a tape recorder with her at all times.

She settled onto the iron chair across from him and set her tape recorder on the table. She raised a questioning brow, a formality since Joe knew she had to do this to understand him.

Joe was already feasting on his cherry Danish. He nodded once, focused on more important things.

"Joe, what do you know about the women who live in the Lady's Home?"

He wiped his mouth and looked keenly at her. "I was meht gnidaeh tuo fo nwot eht rehto thgin. Dah emos dreiw edud htiw meht."

She looked at him and said, "Okay, hang on a moment."

She hit playback on the recorder.

"I saw them heading out of town the other night. Had some weird dude with them."

Sandy looked at him sharply.

"When? And what did this 'weird dude' look like? Where did you see them?"

This time the playback said, "They were down by the Common. They were in that big boat of a car they have. All four of 'em. I saw the man and looked in the window when they were stopped at the light. They flipped out and ran it, almost hitting a truck. Last I saw they were headed west out of town. I'm still hungry."

She went back inside and bought a muffin this time, one that he consumed with alarming speed.

Four pieces of pastry later, Joe was finally full. He tipped his hat to her and gathered himself up, making his way down Main Street on his appointed circuit.

Sandy sat drumming her fingers, her brow furrowed.

She glanced at her watch and jumped up. Jorge was due to arrive in forty-five minutes. Time to get moving.

She glanced after Joe as her mind replayed the information he had given her.

What the hell was going on?

Chapter Twenty-Five

Jim logged onto the computer, casting a wary eye toward Chief Santo's office.

The door remained closed.

The feds hadn't left until some thirty minutes ago, leaving behind his Chief in a sour mood. He had closed himself in his office and put his phone on Do Not Disturb.

Jim was glad of that: he wasn't sure how he would take it if he knew what he was doing.

Logging on, he thought for a moment, his mind making a radius around Brownville that extended some fifty miles. Finally, he typed in a search query highlighting the make and model of their car and waited.

The screen flashed and blinked as the computer searched the database of nationally reported incidents.

Finally, it stopped, with one result listed.

Eagerly he clicked on it.

He read the report twice, his confusion growing. "Attempted Assault with Intent to Murder, Quarry Town, NY.

With growing incredulity, he read of how the owner

of a small gas station had reported how four elderly women in an ancient Buick, no plate given, had threatened to set him ablaze. The station owner had reported he thought they were going to try to rob him but that he was lucky enough to have scared them away with his Alpha manner.

He read the entry a third time.

From Chief Santo's office, he heard motion, then the door opened. Quickly he backed out of the database and logged off. Grabbing his hat and car keys, he left the station.

Brownville drowsed as Jim headed downtown. He scanned the sidewalks, looking for Sandy. Swinging down Elm Street, he rolled past her home.

Her car was gone.

He pulled over and dialed her number. She answered, slightly out of breath.

"Hey, Jim. What's up?"

"Listen, I found something weird here." He told her about the entry in the database he had found.

Sandy was quiet for a moment. "What in the world would they be doing out there? When I saw them the other night, Doris was trying to tell me she was going to see her sister."

"Except she doesn't have one." Jim replied.

"What? That sweet old woman told me a bald faced lie? They have to be involved in Haverill's disappearance."

Jim looked out the driver's side window, his eyes unfocused. "I gotta say, I think they're heading south. I think they're going to D.C."

"But why?" Sandy asked.

"I don't rightly know, but I think they're up to their elbows in something here. And I'm not sure if it's willingly or not. Listen, where are you? We should do some hunting around, see if anyone else can give us an idea of where they may be going."

Sandy was quiet for a moment. Jim heard the distant roar of a motor behind her. "So where are you?" he asked her.

She sighed. "Look, I'm uh, I'm..."

"Sandy?" Jim's eyes had narrowed. "I know this tone."

"Ah shit. I'm sorry Jim. I'm at Hopefield. Jorge Maxim just landed. I'm sorry, but he was sent up here about Haverill."

"Dang it, woman! I wanted to keep this on the down low until we know for certain what's happening." Jim scowled into the phone. This woman drove him nuts sometimes!

"Jimmy, I'm sorry. But Jorge may be the only way we can find them and find out what's going on. And if they ARE being held against their will, then we can find that out too."

"What do you mean 'held against their will'?" he asked in a dangerously quiet tone.

He could hear Jorge's voice faintly saying hello to Sandy. Jim wondered if she was going to answer him or just hang up. He never knew which way she was going to go when it came to a news story.

But she answered him. "I spoke to One Eyed Joe..." and she filled him in about the strange man Joe had seen in the car with the women.

"Why didn't you tell me this?"

"I just DID! And besides, I only saw Joe less than an hour ago." She spoke to Jorge, her voice indistinct. "Listen, honey, Jorge is here, and I need to go. I should fill him in and see if we can make a plan."

"Listen to me." He interjected.

"What is it?" Sandy replied.

"Whatever you two are up to, I'm in it, you understand? Do not go flying out of town without me!"

She was quiet a minute. "You mean that?"

"Do I ever. I've got personal days I can take. Do not leave me out of this, you understand?"

"I... I do. Okay. I'll call you later."

She broke the connection.

Chapter Twenty-Six

"We can't seem to stop anyplace for any reason!" Rita wailed.

"I can't believe this." Lily muttered.

Betty was serene. "They left us alone, didn't they?"

"Betty. You cannot keep threatening people with that THING!" Doris's hands were shaking.

Rita was driving. She slapped her hand on the steering wheel. "We can't keep having people coming over to us like that! We can't!"

"Maybe we should get him a different pair of glasses?" Lily said.

Betty looked over at Ricky. "I think he would look good in those mirrored aviator type ones. He's a very distinguished man you know."

"Yeah well 'distinguished' isn't what we need right now, is it?" Lily replied. "Anonymous would work better if you ask me."

Lily turned to Betty. "So, why'd you bring old Frankie, anyway?"

Betty pursed her lips. "Frankie goes wherever I go. He

always has; he always will."

"Wait...you've been carrying that dick around with you before this?"

"Well of course!"

"How long have you been doing this?" Lily's voice rose.

"Why ever since I brought him home."

Lily and Doris exchanged looks.

"Dare I ask when that was?" Doris asked in a strangled voice.

"Hmmm." Betty looked out the car window, her brow furrowed. "I think it was November or December."

"So, for the past eight or nine months, you've been hauling that THING around wherever you go?" Doris felt faint. They'd gone to a Christmas play together for Pete's sake! With that thing in Betty's bag!

"Oh no, no. I got it last winter, not this past one."

"Oh, holy shit!" Lily stared at her and started to laugh. "You...you had that with you when we went to Sylvia Martin's funeral?" She had died in August of last year.

"Well of course."

"And to Penny's grand-daughter's baptism?" Rita's jaw dropped. "You brought a dildo into the Catholic Church?"

"Well, sure. I wasn't going to leave him home." Betty looked baffled. "Frankie is family."

"Oh my God." Lily covered her face. "You had it with you every place you went." She started laughing. "Please tell me you didn't bring Frankie to confession with you!"

"Of course not!" Betty sniffed. "I left him with Doris while I went in."

Doris's eyes bulged as the memory of pulling Betty's bag next to her hip came to her. Oh, dear God!

Lily burst out laughing. "You had Doris baby sit your

horse dong while you went to confession? Did you confess THAT to Father Ormond while you were at it?"

Betty's lower lip stuck out dangerously. "Frankie is NOT a 'horse dong' as you so inelegantly put it!"

"How big is that thing anyway Betty?" Lily wiped tears from her eyes.

"Frankie is the Deluxe Model, so he measures fourteen inches in length and three and a half inches wide. His trade name was the 'Schlong McDong'. I wasn't going to call him that, so I named him Frankie, after that cute car salesman."

Rita's eyes were round. "The...car salesman? You named it after a guy you dated for a week? I thought you said he was full of crap."

"Oh, he was. But boy he had other attributes to him that I missed, so I went out and found a new and improved Frankie instead. One who doesn't talk. Listening to the real Frankie was the worst part of that relationship."

Doris put her hand to her mouth willing herself not to react. But a small chuckle escaped. Lily lost it when she heard it. All the women started roaring with laughter.

Rita wiped tears off her cheeks.

Doris looked over at the speedometer. "Holy cow, you better slow down! You're doing almost 80!"

Rita glanced down and lifted her foot off the gas pedal.

Behind them there was a burst of red and blue lights.

"Oh shit!" Rita said.

Chapter Twenty-Seven

"What are we going to do?" Doris hissed. "We can't let him see Ricky here. Oh, my land!"

Rita slowed the car and pulled onto the shoulder. Her hand was shaking as she put it in park. "I've never been pulled over before!"

Lily leaned over the seat back. "Just relax. He's going to want your license and registration. With any luck he will let us go."

"With any luck?" Rita moaned.

"What are we going to do about...him?" Doris jerked her head at the rear seat.

Behind them, the police car sat idling, red and blue lights flashing. The silhouette of the officer could be seen inside. He was holding the microphone from the radio to his mouth.

"Oh no, oh no, oh no...." Doris closed her eyes as another wave of faintness hit her.

Betty swiveled around in the seat to look out the rear window. She sighed. "Relax. We will be fine."

Behind them, the officer opened the door and got out. He placed his wide-brimmed hat on his head.

"Relax? Relax? We have a dead man in the car that we had stuffed, and we are supposed to RELAX?" Rita spit. "Oh yeah, I'm going to relax alright."

Boots crunched on the gravel next the car. Warily the officer approached, bending over to cast a look at the occupants. An eyebrow raised when he saw Rita behind the wheel.

"License and registration ma'am."

Doris fumbled with the glove box, spilling napkins and plastic cutlery on the footboards as she opened it.

Rita tugged her paisley bag onto her lap and began to rummage inside of it.

The officer was middle-aged, with prominent lines around his brown eyes. His nose was hooked slightly to one side, a white scar across it visible against his tan.

He eyed them with frank skepticism.

"You mind telling me what the rush is today ma'am?"

He took the offered documents and scanned them.

"I uh, I was...I mean...it was..." Rita stammered.

Lily looked at her with alarm in her eyes. "She's just shaken up, Officer. She's never had a traffic stop before. Hell, this woman's never even gotten a parking ticket."

"Well, I have to say, I was sort of surprised to see this old car traveling at the speed it was. Where are you ladies and gentlemen off to?" His gaze settled on Ricky in the back seat and narrowed.

Oh crap, Doris thought.

"We are trying to get to the Poconos." Betty piped up.

Doris and Rita exchanged astonished looks

"Really. Why are you in such a rush then?" He leaned on the window on folded arms and stared hard at Betty.

She beamed. "Why my beau here can't wait to marry me now, can you?"

The air left Doris's lungs. The black spots danced.

Rita yelped, bringing the officer's attention firmly back to her. He jerked away from the window, his hand slipping to his holster in one move.

"A bee! There's a bee in the car!"

"Oh, geeze Rita. He isn't going to hurt you. Here! Wave him out the window." Lily rolled her eyes. Rita waved her hands as the honeybee buzzed around the front seat. It took flight out her window.

The officer relaxed and leaned against the door once again. He looked back at the rear seat and flushed.

Rita looked in the rear-view mirror and thought she was going to throw up.

Betty had half climbed onto Ricky and was kissing him passionately. One of his arms was around her shoulder; the other had disappeared into her lap.

Lily leaned forward and said, "When you get to be our age, you don't waste any time. These two lovebirds have been canoodling like this for miles."

The officer handed Rita her license and the registration. He eyed her sternly. "I'm going to give you a warning ma'am. You slow down now, you hear? If you get pulled over again, it won't go as well for you." He glanced at the rear seat once more where Betty was cradling Ricky's face in her hands and peppering it with kisses. He shook his head. "And you better get those two to the Poconos as fast as you legally can!" He flushed again. "Good day."

Hitching his belt up, he made his way back to his car.

Doris leaned her head against the headrest and closed her eyes.

Rita reached with her bag with shaking hands, fumbling for her wallet.

In the back seat, Lily looked at Betty who was now trying to give Ricky open-mouthed kisses.

"You can stop now."

Betty moaned slightly and shifted herself further onto Ricky's lap.

"I said you can stop it now Betty!"

The officer pulled past them and accelerated away. Betty continued to moan and grapple with Ricky.

"Rita, let me drive for a while." Doris said. "And Betty, leave that poor man alone!"

"Betty!" Lily grabbed her arm and tugged her hard. She slipped off Ricky's lap and blinked, disoriented. "Betty. It's okay now. You did a great job distracting that cop, but you can stop now."

"Stop?" She looked at Ricky with wide eyes. "Stop? Why?"

"Oh Jesus." Lily muttered. "Rita, we better put her in the front seat for a while.

Doris settled in behind the wheel stiffly as Betty and Rita swapped seats. Rita sidled over against the car door, as far from Ricky as she could get.

"Rita, how much farther do we have to go?"

"About 325 miles."

"How far have we come?"

"About 275 miles."

Doris leaned her head on the steering wheel.

They were never going to get there. Never.

Chapter Twenty-Eight

Jim paced the back hallway of the police station. He peered out the window for the hundredth time.

Chief Santos's car was still there. He shook his head and stepped into the small break room they had.

A 'break room' was probably a generous name for it. It was more like a 'break closet.' He grabbed the coffee pot and sniffed the contents warily. His nose wrinkled as the smell of burnt coffee hit him.

With a sigh he slid it back onto the burner.

Diane Masterson, the senior dispatcher for the Brownville Police appeared in the doorway. Some late fifties, she sported shoulder length ash colored hair, glasses and tired eyes that had seen and heard too much.

"Hey Jimmy." She said as she entered the room. She grabbed the coffee pot.

"I wouldn't bother with that." Jim told her.

She winced as the smell hit her. "Yuck. Doesn't anyone but me make coffee around here?"

Scowling in disgust, she dumped the pot and cleaned it.

As she filled it with fresh water, she glanced out the window.

"Chief's leaving now Jimmy."

"I, uh, what?" Jim stammered as a dull flush rose up his neck.

Diane glanced at him wryly. "You think I haven't been watching you pacing around back here like a caged tiger for the past half hour?"

"Well, uh.. I uh..." he trailed off.

With a laugh, Diane lifted the pot and poured fresh water into the reservoir. The pot hissed and spit. "Relax. I don't care what you're up to. But he's gone now. And none too soon. He's in a foul mood today. Guess he has to go over to the Brickman Motel. Those nasty Feds are staying there."

Jim was already heading into the main room of the station. "I'd be in a foul mood too. Thanks, Diane."

"Uh huh." She said as the door closed.

Jim sat down at his desk and booted up his computer. Tapping in his password, he waited impatiently for the old machine to warm up. He drummed his fingers impatiently on the desk.

At last, it came to life. He clicked through the programs and into the national database. His gaze sharpened when he saw the alert flag in the upper right corner.

Clicking on it, his gaze sharpened when the message filled his screen. His eyes tracked it swiftly.

"Son of a gun." He whispered. He read it a second time.

He pulled his cell phone out and dialed Sandy's number.

Ten minutes later he raced from the station and jumped in his cruiser, leaving a cloud of dust drifting in his wake.

Chapter Twenty-Nine

"Doris. We have to stop for the night." Rita leaned on the seat back. "We can't go any farther, and we've been on the road since early morning."

Outside the countryside rolled past, agonizingly slow. The sun's last rays were barely visible above the hilltops.

Terrified of being pulled over again, Doris had settled at 45 mph, a pace she kept much to the anger of the other motorists on the interstate. Twice tractor trailer trucks had blasted their horns at her as she trundled down the long rolling Pennsylvania hills.

They still had 150 miles to go to Washington D.C.

"I'm hungry!" Betty chimed in. "We haven't eaten today!"

Doris had to admit, she was hungry too.

But they were running out of time. The fundraiser was Saturday night, and it was now Friday evening.

She closed her eyes briefly as her ever present headache throbbed.

Interstate 81 stretched ahead of her, frustratingly potholed or slowed by miles of road construction.

They weren't even to Harrisburg yet.

Lily was peering out the car window as a sign announcing the next exit's attractions loomed.

"Let's get off here. There's a couple of hotels, chain hotels. Those should be okay."

Rita wrinkled her nose. "I hate to say it, but I think Ricky here is starting to smell."

"What?" Doris's head whipped around. "I thought the whole point of taxidermy was to prevent that!"

"Hey, Hiram did the best he could, given the circumstances. YOU were the one who wanted it done in one day!" Lily was indignant.

"I was the one who wanted to get bags of ice!"

"I still say we should have just called the police." Rita muttered. "We could have avoided all of this mess!"

Lily's shoulders slumped. She exchanged a look with Doris.

"That wasn't an option, Rita." She told her.

Rita sniffed. "I still say we should have. She didn't do anything wrong!"

"Maybe not legally, but morally." Doris replied.

"It's not up to her to police other people." Rita's jaw was set.

Lily leaned around Ricky to pin Rita with a stare. "Did you really want to see her sent away to one of those places? To be dragged through the media? Do you have ANY idea what a circus it would have been?" She looked at Ricky. "If it had been ANYONE other than HIM, yes, calling the police would have been the right thing to do. But not when it was him."

"Oh, and how do you think it's going to go when they find out their candidate for Vice President of the United

States is dead and has been taxidermized?" Rita's voice was rising.

Doris shook her head as she took the off ramp. "Not our problem then."

"Until it comes back on us!" Rita yelled.

Betty started to cry. "I didn't mean to kill him!"

"Now Betty, you didn't kill him. He died of natural causes. But you can't keep bringing men home like that!" Doris glanced at her worriedly. "Look at the mess it made!"

"But...but I LIKE men!"

"Isn't...isn't that Frankie enough for you?"

"I love Frankie, but I need variety!"

Rita and Lily exchanged looks. Lily leaned forward. "Tell you what," she said, "You stop bringing these men home and we will take you over to Rangely. You can buy two, hell three more and name them all different names. You can have a new man every night. Maybe even buy one of those electric tongues while you're at it, for a change of pace."

"Lily!" Doris flushed, aghast. "An electric...WHAT?"

Ahead the yellow lights of the first chain hotel glowed.

"Oh, come now Doris. Don't tell me you don't know about the things they sell in those stores. They have dildos, tongues, butt plugs, ball gags..."

"WHAT?" Doris and Rita gasped in unison. "How in Sam Hill do YOU know about those things?"

Lily had the grace to flush a little. "Well, you know, sometimes I had to go get gag gifts for showers and stuff."

"After seeing the size of that thing she has, I bet they were gag gifts." Rita muttered.

Doris pulled into the lot of the hotel and parked the car. She rubbed her face as exhaustion hit her.

Butt plugs...ball gags. Good lord. She had no idea what either of those things were.

And she sure as hell didn't want to find out.

Straightening up she looked across the parking lot to the lobby. This hotel was a national chain, and there were a lot of cars in the parking lot.

She turned to Rita. "I'll go in and get a room. I think we are far enough away from the building that we can get him into the cart without anyone noticing."

Wincing, she pulled herself out of the car and started shuffling toward the lobby.

The clerk was polite but disinterested in her as she registered. He handed her two key cards and instructions on where the elevators were, and when breakfast was served.

Palming the key cards, she pushed her way back out into the night. Rain was starting to spit. She could see the others by the car, fussing over the pile on the cart.

She had to admit, it was an awkward looking pile of luggage.

Lily muttered a curse as a wheel hit a hole in the parking lot, causing her bag to tumble off the heap. "Dag nab it! That's the second time! You'd think they'd spend some money on their parking lot."

Rita was tugging on the front of the cart. "Come on. Another ten feet and we will be on the sidewalk."

Doris grabbed the other front handle as Betty pushed weakly on the rear. "I saw a restaurant around the building. We can walk to it."

Eagerly, they pushed the teetering cart onto the sidewalk and rolled it toward the lobby.

Rita frowned when she spotted the shiny gold luggage carts the chain used. Their shabby silver one stood out like a sore thumb.

Lily rotated the cart as they reached the doors, backing through them.

They entered the lobby.

The clerk was checking a young couple in as they entered. He glanced up, then away then back again. His brow furrowed in bewilderment when he saw their cart.

"Evening!" Lily called out.

The young couple glanced over their shoulders at them; a smile crossed the woman's face. Her partner raised an eyebrow and smirked.

"So much for staying anonymous." Doris hissed.

The pushed and pulled the creaking cart through the lobby and around the corner into the hallway. The elevators were some twenty feet down the hall.

"What floor are we..." Lily started to say as the cart's front wheel caught a seam in the carpet.

Rita was pushing hard from behind when it happened. The cart turned suddenly and tipped, spilling the contents all over the hallway, knocking Doris down in the process.

Ricky slid off and lay there still in his seated position from the car seat, his hat three feet away, the glasses knocked sideways off his face.

His huge brown bear eyes stared glassily at nothing, the hall lights reflecting in them.

"SHIT!" Lily hissed. "Doris! Are you okay?"

Doris pulled herself up into a sitting position, willing the pain in her hip to stop. "Don't worry about me! Get him covered up!"

Rita and Betty scrambled after the spilled bags as Lily grabbed Ricky's arm. She heaved on him, dragging his head and shoulders back onto the cart.

"Never mind the bags! Help me out here!"

From around the corner, they heard voices as the couple who had just checked in headed to the elevators.

There was a ping from the elevator as the button on the next floor up glowed. The arrow pointed down: it would be at the lobby momentarily.

Doris felt her throat closing up. She hauled herself up off the floor and grabbed Ricky's arm as Betty and Rita dropped the bags. Together the four women wiggled him back onto the cart, just as the couple cleared the corner into the hallway.

Lily grabbed Betty's bag and heaved it unceremoniously on top of Ricky. Rita dragged her bag onto his thighs. Betty struggled with Doris's bag, dragging it onto the end of the cart.

"You need a hand there?" The young man smiled at them. He had olive skin and dark hair, very fit and trim. His partner was petite and well dressed. She too had dark hair, brushing her shoulders, with subtle makeup and large eyes. A small smirk played around the corner of her mouth.

Doris looked at the cart as they drew closer, and her heart stopped.

Ricky's lower legs were uncovered and were very clearly human legs.

She grabbed the handle on the end of the cart and half collapsed down on top of the body, her knees folded over his legs. She plunked her purse on his feet.

Lily jumped and gaped at her wide eyed. Rita and Betty stared with open astonishment.

"I'm tired. I think I'll ride up."

Lily looked at her then at the couple. "We're okay, thanks. Just had a little tumble is all."

She stepped forward and grabbed her bag. "We can just carry this one up so you can ride."

Betty and Rita exchanged looks, but mercifully said nothing.

Doris squared her shoulders and lifted her chin. She strove for a blasé attitude, as if they did this all the time.

Amusement wrinkled the corners of the young man's eyes. His partner turned away as the elevator door opened, disgorging an older man. He did a double take at the women, staring openly.

The young man held the elevator door. "Here. Why don't you take this one."

The women pushed and shoved the cart onto the elevator, struggling with Doris's weight and with how unbalanced it now was.

Lily gave them a big grin as they sidled the cart sideways in the elevator.

"Thank you kindly! It's always a pleasure to meet people who aren't acting like we have a body in our luggage."

The young woman laughed out loud as the elevator doors started sliding shut. They heard her say to her partner as the doors closed,

"Oh my gosh, weren't they sweet? Those old ladies are a riot!"

Doris put her face in her hands.

Rita leaned against the wall, her face ashen.

"What floor are we on?" Lily asked.

Doris handed her the key wordlessly. Lily pressed the button.

The doors slid open to the third floor. Lily checked the hallway. Finding it empty, they wiggled and shoved the cart out of the elevator. Doris reached for Rita's hand using it to help pull herself upright. They shoved Lily's bag onto Ricky's feet and made their way to room 311.

They struggled through it and slammed it shut, locking every dead bolt and chain.

Doris sank down into the upholstered chair next to one of the beds. Her hands were shaking violently.

Rita dropped her purse on the bed and sat down heavily next to it. She looked at Lily. "Do you think you could please stop telling everyone we have a corpse on the luggage cart?"

Lily grinned. "You gotta understand something about human nature. If I didn't say we had a body with us, they would wonder if we had one. If I say everyone thinks we have one, they think, 'oh they must not have one' and they don't think for a second that we do."

Betty pulled the desk chair out and slumped down into it. "What kind of screwed up, twisted line of logic is that?"

Lily shrugged. "It's humans. If you openly tell them something, they won't believe you. If you try to hide it, they start thinking you are doing something." She looked at the luggage cart speculatively. "You know, the cart seemed like a good plan, but I think we may need to do something better."

"Like what?" Doris asked.

Chapter Thirty

Sandy, Jorge and Jim sped along Interstate 81 following the twin taillights of the black Ford Explorer some twenty car lengths ahead of them. They had been tailing them for several hours now as they flew across the darkened landscape, driving well over the speed limit.

Many miles had slid behind them as they plunged through the darkness of New York State.

"Are you sure they are following them?" Sandy asked again.

In the back seat, Jorge's face was lit by the glow of the iPad as he followed the track of the car in front of them. Apparently, his budget had included the funds necessary for slipping a tracking device in the wheel well of the car the two obnoxious Feds were driving.

"Case, they peeled out of that motel like they were on fire. They're after them. I'd bet my career on it."

They had almost caught them in the act of sticking the tracker on the car. One minute, things were quiet and then the motel door had slammed open spilling light across the lot as the two Feds had tumbled out in a dead run. Jorge, who was just backing away from the car when it happened, had resorted to rolling beneath an old work van as they raced down the sidewalk.

Sandy and Jim had a stomach dropping moment thinking they had spotted Jorge, but they had piled into the car and peeled out instead.

Clearly something had happened that caused their rapid exit from Brownville.

They headed west at a high rate of speed.

Jorge fussed with the oil stain on his right sleeve again. "I swear, Case. Every time I have to work with you, my wardrobe suffers."

Sandy snorted. "I suspect you can afford to replace that shirt, Jorge."

Jorge sighed. "I suppose you're right, but I do like this one." He said sadly.

Jim tried to push aside the worry about what would happen if, or rather when, they found the tracker.

"We're going to have to stop. What happens when we do?" Sandy fretted.

"Case, you worry too much. They can run, but they can't hide." Jorge's voice was serene.

Jim had his own private doubts about that, but he kept them to himself.

"Tell me again what One Eyed Joe told you." He said to Sandy.

She sighed. "The story hasn't changed, Jim. For the third time..."

"Fourth actually." Jorge chimed in from the back seat.

"Fourth time, he saw a weird looking man in the car with them, a big man. He said they seemed rattled and even ran a red light."

"They're in trouble, I just know it." Jim muttered. "I've known those ladies since I was little, and they would never do anything bad. Someone is making them do this."

"Maybe that's the case." Jorge replied. "But for some reason, the Feds are awfully interested in them as well."

Sandy tapped her teeth with a pen and looked at the path the Explorer was taking. She checked the map. "Jim, they have to be heading to Harrisburg. They can't possibly get any further than that tonight. IF they haven't stopped already and IF they are even going this way."

Jim nodded toward the Explorer. "Those fellas seem mighty sure of which way they're going."

Sandy frowned. "How can they know that? That's an old car they're driving, so it's not like they can track it using its GPS unit."

Jorge didn't look up from the glowing screen he held. "Traffic cameras." He said.

"Huh?" Sandy swiveled around in the seat and eyed him narrowly. "How can they get the information that quickly?"

"It's elementary. They're working for someone high enough up in the food chain that when they ask, people jump. That car is distinctive enough that a simple search in the computer system will trigger alerts every time that make and model is detected." He finally looked up from his iPad. "And there's a good possibility they are the only ones in this area in one of those cars right now."

Sandy turned around and settled back into her seat. "That's just creepy."

"That's just the digital age, Case."

Chapter Thirty-One

"I don't like this. She should have been back by now!" Rita wrung her hands as she paced.

"Just relax. Lily's resourceful." Doris didn't want to admit that she too was getting worried. And hungry. It had been an hour since Lily took the keys to the Buick and left.

Periodically, voices echoed down the hallway as people made their way to their room. Each voice made them cringe.

As an hour and twenty minutes passed since Lily's departure, they heard 'tap tap' on the door.

Rita whirled and strode over to the door. She pressed her eye to the peephole.

"She's back!" She fumbled with the chain and deadbolt. Betty and Doris crowding in behind her.

She opened the door to Lily, who was smiling broadly. She had a wheelchair in front of her with brown paper bags stacked on the seat. And she was wearing a pair of silver mirrored aviator glasses.

The bags smelled awfully good.

"I have returned!" She pushed the chair into the room.

"And I stopped and got dinner for us. I didn't get anything for him." She jerked her head at Ricky.

Doris bit her tongue. She wasn't sure about Lily's idea, not at all, but clearly the luggage cart wasn't working out as well as they'd hoped.

Betty took the bags and set them on the desk. She started opening them. "Hey, what's this for?" She pulled out a New York Yankees baseball cap and frowned at it.

Lily had taken the sunglasses off. "That's for Ricky too. That hat just makes him look weird."

"He LOOKS weird. I sure hope Hiram isn't planning on doing more jobs like this one." Rita shivered.

Lily scowled. "Come on. Help me get him up."

Betty pulled a hooded sweatshirt out of the bag. It sported an ad for an energy drink on the front. "Is this for Ricky too?"

"Yup! Sometimes hiding something in plain sight is the best way to hide. Come on; give me a hand here."

"He could probably use one of those drinks right about now." Rita said dryly.

They wrestled Ricky off the cart and into the chair, where Lily set about getting the sweatshirt on him and adjusting his arms and legs.

She zipped it up. "There. Now, watch this."

She placed the sunglasses on his face, then the ball cap.

"Ta da!" She stepped back, pleased with her work.

Doris had to admit; he looked better this way.

Lily reached for the red sunglasses. "We need to give these back to Hiram when we get home."

Betty's shoulders slumped. "You mean IF we get home."

"WHEN we get home." Doris said sternly. "Stop thinking like that. This will work. It HAS to."

She refused to allow the nagging worry in her head a voice.

She looked at Ricky and looked away with a shudder. He may have looked better, but he still didn't look right.

Lily and Rita unloaded the bags of food onto the desk as Betty sat back down on the side of one of the beds. She stared at Ricky, a wistful expression on her face.

Lily turned and caught sight of her.

"Oh no you don't! Uh uh. Stop staring at him like that!"

Betty's lower lip protruded dangerously. "Stop being mean to me!"

"I'll stop being mean to you when you stop getting us in a jam, lady!"

"Hey, hey now!" Rita interjected. "Stop it you two!"

"She started it!" Betty pouted.

Rita sighed and caught Doris's eye. She rolled hers.

"Betty." Doris said. "How about you eat dinner now, and then you and Rita can go downstairs and use their computers. Rita, can you check the schedule and make sure they are still holding this gala tomorrow?" She felt faint thinking about what would happen if they canceled it.

Rita was scooping pasta out of a container onto a plate. She nodded. "We can do that, right Betty?"

Betty didn't answer, but she got up and came over to the food.

Lily piled her plate with salad and pasta and came over to perch on the edge of the upholstered chair.

Doris leaned over to her. "Can you please STOP antagonizing her?" she whispered.

Lily snorted derisively her mouth full. She swallowed and whispered back, "Doris, she's not right!"

"I know that, but that's a problem for tomorrow not tonight."

Rita handed Doris a plate. She accepted it wearily.

The women fell silent as they ate. Lily stared at Ricky. "You know, I think this will work. I think we can just walk right in with him like this and no one will even look twice."

Rita sighed. "I hope to hell you're right, Lily."

Rita finished her meal and tossed her plate in the trash. She wiped her mouth. "Ready Betty?"

Betty nodded and got up, tossing her plate in the trash. "Wait. I have to brush my teeth first."

"Hurry up." Rita called to her. She mumbled something then emerged a moment later wiping her mouth. The two women exited the room.

Lily gathered up the remnants of the meal and stuffed it back into the bags. Doris picked up the television remote and frowned at it.

"I swear they make these more complicated than they need to be."

Lily held out her hand. "Here. Let me try."

She fiddled with the buttons and the set bloomed to life.

"There you go." She said, handing the remote back to Doris.

Doris was staring at the television, her mouth hanging open.

On the screen a newscaster was talking urgently. The screen behind him was filled with a photo of a man exiting a black limousine, his wife behind him.

The banner scrolling beneath the photo read "Mystery of candidates whereabouts deepens."

The man in the photo was Ricky Haverill.

Chapter Thirty-Two

Time froze.

Doris fumbled with the remote, raising the volume. Beside her Lily muttered, "Oh crap."

They watched in silence as the newscaster relayed the story of Ricky Haverill's odd disappearance from public view after last being seen in New Hampshire, and about how his party was stonewalling the press.

They closed by talking about the upcoming gala in DC and how they wondered if he would make an appearance there, and what it would mean if he didn't.

The segment ended, and they moved on to the latest indiscretion by a congressman. Doris fumbled with the remote, shutting the television off.

They sat in stunned silence for a moment.

The door key rattled, making them both jump. Rita pushed the door open and rushed in, followed by a worried looking Betty.

"We have a problem!" she blurted.

"I know. We just saw it on the news." Doris replied woodenly.

"What do you mean you just saw it on the news?" Rita's voice climbed several octaves.

Doris looked at her. "Aren't you talking about Ricky's disappearance?"

"What? Well, no, I mean yes, but no. Why? What was on the news?"

Lily drew a breath. "Cat's out of the bag. The press is reporting Ricky is AWOL."

"Was that all they said?" Rita asked urgently.

"Well...yes. Wasn't that enough?" Lily shot back.

Rita shook her head. "We have a bigger problem than that!"

Doris and Lily looked at her in concern. Betty was wringing her hands. "I decided to check my email while we were on the computer. I haven't looked at it in days. There was an email there from that horrid Sandy Case."

"Sandy Case?" Doris's brow furrowed. "What's she got to do with this?"

"She told me she knows I was involved in the disappearance of Ricky Haverill and said that if I didn't get back to her in twenty four hours, she was going to go to the Feds about it. That they could and would track us down no matter how far we ran. And if they didn't, she would."

"What?" Lily burst out. "She wouldn't do that...would she?"

"Betty, when did this email come in?" Doris's throat was tight.

"Yesterday afternoon."

Yesterday afternoon was more than 24 hours ago.

"Oh shit!" Lily said. "She won't really do that, will she?"

"It's Sandy Case. She's liable to do anything." Rita said grimly.

"She has no proof of anything." Doris said. "She's trying to scare you."

"She sent a picture with it." Betty raised her hand to her mouth. Her eyes glistened.

"A picture of what?" Doris stared at her.

"Of m-me and Ricky g-getting into the c-car." She started sobbing.

"The...car?" Doris repeated dumbly. "The CAR? The car we are DRIVING?"

Betty nodded.

"She has a PICTURE of YOU AND RICKY getting into our BUICK?"

Tears spilled down Betty's face. She nodded.

"Where in the WORLD did she get that?"

"It looked like security camera footage." Rita replied.

They stared at each other as the realization of what had happened washed over them.

"The car." Doris said softly. "We can't use it anymore."

"But how are we going to get to Washington? We can't give up our car!" Lily burst out.

Rita paced across the room and pulled the corner of the curtain back. She peered at the dark lot. "Nuts. I can't see it from here."

Doris rubbed both hands over her face. "Okay. Think. Just slow down and think a moment here."

They fell silent.

She dropped her hands and looked at them. "Rita did you get a chance to check on the gala? The news said it was still going on, but I don't know if I believe that."

"It's still on as far as I can tell." She replied.

"And it's been over twenty four hours and we've seen no one suspicious, no one following us?"

They exchanged worried looks.

"Well, I wasn't really watching for that, were you?" Lily asked.

Doris slapped her knees in frustration. "Damn it all! Damn that woman!"

"What are we going to do?" Betty wailed.

"I don't know!" Doris snapped.

Lily had started pacing as they talked. She stopped now, a far-away look in her eyes.

"I think I have an idea." She said.

Chapter Thirty-Three

"We are wasting so much money!" Rita hissed as they hurried through the mercifully empty hallway of the hotel. "That room cost a pretty penny!"

Ricky was ensconced in his wheelchair, aviator glasses in place, Doris's bag in his lap. The cart had been left abandoned in the room.

"Shush. That's the least of our worries." Doris replied. She grimaced and tried to ignore the pain searing through her hip.

Betty was silent, grimly dragging her and Lily's bag behind her.

"She's going to be there, right?" Rita asked worriedly. "What if something goes wrong?"

"It won't." Doris replied curtly.

The elevator was maddeningly slow. Betty fidgeted, looking around the hall nervously.

"Come on." Doris said as the door slid open.

They descended to the first floor where they stopped

with a slight bounce. The door sighed back open. Rita poked her head out.

No Lily.

Doris gestured with her head. "Come on, go. We'll wait outside around the back like she said to."

"What if the feds are there?" Rita asked.

"They won't be, now go!"

A young Black woman sauntered around the corner just then, adjusting a sling bag on her shoulder. She stopped in front of the elevator waiting to get on.

Nervously Doris pushed Ricky out into the lobby, studiously avoiding meeting the woman's eye. She raised her eyebrow when she saw his sunglasses, and looked at the women, but said nothing.

Rita, Doris and Betty clustered together in a tight clump, scurrying for the door, Ricky leading the way.

To Doris it felt like they were pushing an elephant through the room.

The desk was empty.

Like a school of worried fish, they pushed their way out of the brightly lit lobby and into the late night. Pools of light glowed under parking lot lamps. At this hour, most of the rooms were dark.

"Are we sure she even got one? Who is open this hour of the night?" Rita gnawed on her thumb distractedly.

"She said they called, and that they were open. They were supposed to send someone for her." Doris repeated grimly. "Just wait."

They stopped by the side of the building, where the rooms above gave way to conference rooms.

Rita waved at an insect banging off of her face.

"Where IS she?"

Betty was peeking around the corner of the building. "Someone just pulled in." she said excitedly. "Maybe it's her!"

The other two women sidled over to the edge of the building to look.

The black Ford Explorer idled through the lot, up and down each row.

They stopped in the back lot.

Next to the Buick.

Light flickered on as the doors opened. Even from here they could see two people getting out.

Doris put her hand over her mouth.

"Holy..." Rita said.

Betty was staring open-mouthed. "She did it. That rotten woman did it."

"Psst! Hey!" The whisper came from behind them, making them jump.

Doris felt faint as black spots danced in her vision.

Lily had come from behind the building.

"Come on! I'm back here. There're some Fed types over there. I saw them turn in, so I went around. Let's get out of here!"

They ran as fast as Ricky and their luggage allowed. Lily had parked at the loading dock of the hotel, the big UHaul van emblazoned with RENT ME! $19.95 a day!

She opened the back door, and they unceremoniously hauled Ricky out of his chair and into the van. His folding chair was shoved in on top of him.

They threw their luggage in behind him and piled in. Lily took off and streaked out the back entrance of the lot, throwing them around like rag dolls.

"Geeze!" Betty said, clinging to the bench seat. "We aren't buckled in yet!"

"Never mind that! Just go!" Doris said.

Lily needed no encouragement. She went.

Chapter Thirty-Four

"Hey look! They're getting off!"

Sandy leaned forward, wincing as her back protested the hours they had spent in the car. Traveling at times at triple digit speed, they had covered the same mileage in a fraction of the time it had taken Doris, who had crept along at less than half their pace.

Ahead of them, the black Ford Explorer had slowed abruptly, brake lights glowing brightly. It swerved down the ramp.

Jorge leaned forward his face intent. "Take the second exit. It's only a quarter of a mile up. We can't have them spotting us!"

"But we are going to lose them!" Sandy wailed.

"No, we are not! Now, Case, relax and trust me. The next exit, Jim."

"Got it." Jim's jaw was set. The Explorer pulled off into the exit ramp. He swept past them and took the next one.

"Turn left at the bottom of the ramp. They pulled into that hotel just down the street."

The hotel's lights reflected off the black Explorer as it slowly drove through the parking lot.

Jorge leaned forward. "Don't turn in here; go around the building and in the service entrance. There. Take a right onto Dunstable Road."

Jim swung the car into the road that ran behind the hotel. Sandy looked out the passenger side window and did a double take.

"Holy shit! There they are!"

Across the lot, the four women were hustling along at an alarmingly fast pace for them, and even more surprisingly, they were pushing someone in a wheelchair.

"What the hell?" Jorge said, craning to see them out the window.

Jim muttered a curse. There was no way into the parking lot from here.

"Where's the dang entrance?" he shouted.

"You have to take a right up there." Jorge countered.

The women had reached a UHaul van and were disappearing into it at a shocking speed. The lights flared on it, and it peeled away from the loading dock with twin puffs of tire smoke, ripping out of the parking lot as Jim made the turn onto the road behind the hotel.

"Nothing for it now but to follow them." Jim said.

"They must have seen the Feds." Jorge replied.

"Apparently, they figured that out before. That was a UHaul they got into, not their car." Jim said. A small smile played around his lips. "There may be snow on the roofs, but there's still fire in the hearth."

"What?" Sandy asked.

He shook his head. "Nothing. Just an old family saying. Keep a sharp eye on 'em. We don't have a tracker on them."

Jorge looked at the iPad. "They Feds are still at the hotel. They aren't moving now."

Jim's voice was grim. "But they will be."

"Just don't lose that UHaul." Sandy told him.

"I won't. I know how to track." Jim said.

Traffic was light but steady on the highway. Jim kept pace with the van, dropping back at times and moving up at others. They reached a bottleneck from construction. Sandy peered around the car in front of them at the white roof of the UHaul, some three vehicles ahead.

"They have their turn signal on." She said.

The van turned down off the highway into a light industrial area and slowly made its way down a divided two-lane road peppered with traffic lights every couple of blocks. Jim was forced to edge closer to the van so they wouldn't lose it.

Sandy fretted that the women would see them, but the van gave no indication the driver was aware of them.

Jorge glanced at the iPad screen. "The Feds are still at the hotel."

"Why would they stay there?" Sandy asked.

"If'n that were me, I'd impound the car and process it." Jim replied. "They mighta lost 'em but they'll figger out right quick that they have another car."

"Here's hoping the hotel doesn't have many cameras in back of it." Jorge muttered.

"Where are they going?" Sandy asked as the van swung down a side street. It slowed even more, then stopped in front of a small ranch house.

They pulled in behind them.

"They're going to bolt." Sandy said.

"They're a bunch of old ladies, Case." Jorge said.

"Old ladies who happen to be involved in the disappearance of a candidate for the Vice Presidency of the United States." She replied acidly.

"They're getting out." Jim grabbed the door handle. "Stay here and let me handle it."

The driver's side and passenger side doors on the UHaul opened and two college-aged men slid out. They glanced at the car with curiosity as they stretched.

"What the heck?" Jim snapped. He pushed his door open. "Hey! You two! Stop right there! Police!"

"What the hell, man?" The driver, a skinny young man with glasses and a soul patch looked at Jim with alarm. "We didn't do anything!"

His passenger was a chubby red-head whose face was clean shaven but still ravaged with the telltale signs of acne. "Come on! What's your problem? This is my parent's house!"

"Who else is with you?" Jim strode toward them, his voice suspicious.

"With us? No one is with us. We're coming back from dropping Eddie's sister off at Cornell. Here..." the driver threw the side door open.

Other than fast food bags and sleeping bags, the van was empty.

Jim sagged. "I'm sorry. We have the wrong vehicle. Sorry to bother you fellas." He started backing away.

"Hey, you said you were a cop! Let me see some ID!" the red head barked.

"Have a good night." Jim slid into the car and swung away from the curb.

The red head flipped him off.

"I don't understand what happened!" Sandy said.

Jorge's face was grim. "We followed the wrong van off the highway is what happened."

"Shit! How are we going to find them again?" she replied.

Jorge shook his head. "We aren't. But I think I might have an idea about where they are going."

Chapter Thirty-Five

"I'm tired." Betty complained from the back seat. "Can't we stop some place and rest for a bit?"

Lily was driving, still hopped up on adrenaline, even though hours had passed since their narrow escape.

She shook her head no. "Just be quiet and get some sleep. We can't stop now Betty. We should be in D.C. soon."

Doris wearily raised her head, blinking as she came awake. The van was rough to ride in, every bump and jolt shooting through her. "We need to figure out what we are going to do when we get there."

Outside the night was grudgingly giving way to daylight. The UHaul van moved along in a light stream of traffic, completely invisible to other drivers.

Doris had to admit; Lily was right about hiding in plain sight.

The state of Maryland rolled past in the predawn light. Washington D.C. was some 30-odd miles south of their location. Doris hoped the traffic stayed light; she was more than ready to be out of this van. More than ready to be home in Brownville, enjoying her tea in the kitchen.

She wondered if they would ever get to do that again.

Pushing that worry aside, she asked Rita, "Where did you say the event was being held tonight?"

Rita stifled a yawn and rubbed her face. Her normally coiffed hair hung lank and straight to her shoulders. They all looked worse for wear after the long night of no sleep and running away.

"It's at the Capitol Regency Hotel. It's a swanky looking place within walking distance of the Capitol." She raised her hand and absently gnawed on her thumb. "How are we going to do this?" she asked.

"Can we get a room in the same hotel and just move him down the hallway?" Lily asked.

Doris shook her head no. "I doubt there will be any rooms open and even if they were, I know we can't afford one."

They fell silent.

The van's tires hissed as another mile fell behind them.

"Well, what if we just smuggled him in and left him someplace in the hotel? They'd find him, eventually." Lily said.

"If the press finds him first, all hell will break loose." Betty said grimly. "We have to leave him where his campaign finds him, not the public."

"Why?" Lily asked.

"Because they aren't going to want this to get out." Betty answered. "If anyone can spin this and kill any press, it's going to come from them."

"Boy, I don't know about that." Rita said. "How do we know they won't blow it up? Then we will have everyone looking for us! Not just the Feds!"

Doris closed her eyes a moment. Dear Lord. How had her life come to this?

She opened them again and squared her shoulders. "Let's keep going. We will look for a place we can afford as close to the hotel as we can. We can figure it out from there."

"We need to stop." Rita said. "We haven't slept, we are all hungry and I for one could use a bathroom! We can figure out what to do over breakfast."

"I think that's a great idea." Betty said.

"There's a Waffle House off the next exit." Rita said as the exit services sign rolled past them.

Doris pursed her lips. Breakfast DID sound tempting, but she was worried about leaving Ricky lying in the back. Every time they left him some place it seemed like trouble followed.

She said as much to them.

Lily shrugged. "Then we take him inside with us."

Doris's head whipped around, her mouth hanging. "We...WHAT? Are you insane?"

"Trust me. No one will take a second look at him."

"And if they DO?"

"They won't." Lily put her blinker on and moved into the exit lane. "People never see what's right under their noses."

They swept down the ramp where the square yellow letters glowed with the promise of bacon, eggs pancakes, coffee and hopefully, a plan.

Chapter Thirty-Six

"Good morning. Five for breakfast?"

The young woman sported a ring in her nose, short messy brown hair and an air of indifference.

Doris clung to the handles of the wheelchair Ricky was in, feeling faint.

Dear God.

"Yes ma'am!" Lily beamed at her. "We sure are ready for some coffee and hotcakes."

The woman's eyes glazed over worse than the three day old donuts on the counter.

"This way."

They followed her through the restaurant, which was far busier at this hour than they cared to see. A few people glanced at them then turned their attention back to the food at hand.

No one looked twice at Ricky.

The woman glanced over her shoulder and waved them to a booth with a handicap sticker on the end of it. There was ample room to sidle Ricky up to the table and still allow the women to slide in on both sides of the table.

Lily looked at her. "Can you bring a pot of coffee and five mugs please?"

"Um hm." She scribbled it down and left.

Rita cast a nervous look at Ricky sitting at the head of the table. "Are we really supposed to eat with him watching us like that?"

Doris had to admit, it was on the creepy side. She was seated closest to him on his right, with Rita beside her. Lily and Betty sat across from her, with Lily next to him. She glanced over at him casually. "You gotta admit; it's nice to sit down to a meal with a man who doesn't say anything."

Betty snorted. "Lily!"

Rita frowned at her. "Well, I don't find it nice at all!"

Doris picked up the menu. "Can we focus on the food please? We need food and we need an idea."

They fell silent for a moment.

The waitress returned and thunked a white plastic pot of coffee down and a tray with mugs and condiments. She plucked her pad out of her apron. "You folks ready to order?"

They went around the table from Doris, ending with Lily who ordered a stack of pancakes with sausage for herself and a hungry man's breakfast special for Ricky.

Rita's eyes widened.

The waitress scribbled the order down then looked fully at Ricky for the first time. A slight frown crossed her lips.

"Hey, your friend here alright?" She jerked her chin at him.

"Why of course he is." Lily replied brightly.

"He's like...not moving or nothing." She looked dubious.

"Oh he's asleep." Lily replied. "He has narcolepsy, so he falls asleep at the drop of a hat, and he carries his own hat."

"Huh?" the girl's brow furrowed.

"It's an old saying. Never mind." Doris interjected.

"Huh. Wow, okay, cool. I'll get your order in then."

She gathered up the menus and departed.

Rita, Doris and Betty exchanged looks. Doris leaned forward and hissed, "What are you doing ordering food for him? You don't think it's not going to look suspicious if we send back an entire plate?"

Lily shrugged. "It's gonna look worse if we don't. We can split his meal between us. I don't know about you, but I'm starved."

They fell silent for a few moments looking around the room. A few tables were occupied, and about half the counter. It was early, still predawn. A couple of tractor-trailer rigs idled in the lot. Pickup trucks accounted for the bulk of the rest.

The food arrived carried by a young man who was even more disinterested in them than the waitress had been. They dug in.

Doris had to admit; she was famished.

Periodically, Lily would glance around then steal something off Ricky's plate. She dropped the morsels on everyone's plates, doling them out until his plate was emptied.

As they ate, Lily paused and opened her purse. Rummaging around in it, she came out with a map of Washington D.C.

She folded it back to the area they needed and spread it on the table. She tapped on a square just off from the street the Capitol was on.

"That's where we have to go."

They fell silent a moment staring at the location. Seeing

it so close to the Capitol of the country brought it home for them.

"What time does the event start?" Doris asked breaking their reverie.

"Oh, um, hang on." Rita pulled her bag around and rummaged in it. She pulled out a pad of paper. "Seven o'clock."

Doris looked across the restaurant to the wall clock.

"So that gives us slightly less than fifteen hours." She said grimly.

Betty looked at Ricky as she nibbled on the edge of her toast. "How are we going to do this?"

Rita pursed her lips. "I suppose we could go in and use one of their luggage carts and move him in that way, like we did at the motel."

Lily was already shaking her head. "No. No that's not going to work. We take him inside in his chair."

Doris was aghast. "We can't do that!"

Lily looked at her with one brow raised. "And why can't we?"

"Because we will be walking into a hotel filled with people who have been looking for him all week, that's why!"

Lily cocked her head. "You really haven't learned anything about hiding in plain sight now, have you?"

"Not when we are trying to roll him through a room full of Secret Service and other people who are trained in looking for things like this!"

Betty let a small smile play around her mouth as the waitress made her way back across the restaurant to them. "I've got a plan."

Chapter Thirty-Seven

The new motel was dingy and brown.

Rita wrinkled her nose at the stale scent of long-ago smoked cigarettes as they wheeled Ricky in over the threshold.

Doris fanned the air in front of her face and Betty tugged fruitlessly on the window trying to open it.

"Geeze. This place is like Fifty Shades of Beige." Lily announced, turning to take it all in.

"Oh lord." Rita snorted, her hand covering her nose.

Outside downtown Washington D.C. hummed and rattled, the noise penetrating the walls of the ancient motel. The Regency was far beyond their limited means, so they had done the next best, or maybe next closest thing; a room at this tired no-tell motel a few blocks from the glitz and glamor, right on the ragged edge of the really seedy part of the city.

They looked at Ricky sitting in next to the desk, still clad in his hat, aviator sunglasses and energy drink sweatshirt.

Rita sank down on the threadbare, saggy bed. She

looked around the room. "How are we supposed to sleep in here? It's only got one bed."

"With any luck, we won't have to." Lily replied. She looked at Betty. "Are you ready to do our reconnaissance?"

Betty nodded. "Let me just freshen up a bit first." She headed into the bathroom.

Doris wrung her hands. "Are you sure?" she called into the bathroom.

"I'm sure." Betty's voice was muffled by the cheap hollow-core door.

Lily stretched and smiled at Doris. "If anyone knows how these things work, it's Betty."

The bathroom door opened, and Betty emerged, patting her lips with a tissue. "I had to freshen my makeup." She said.

Lily rolled her eyes. "The last time I wore any makeup was in 2010 when I went to Agatha's wedding. And what a waste that was! They were divorced by 2012."

Betty dropped her lipstick back in her bag. "Well, you better be ready to wear it again because you're going to have to tonight."

"Oh brother." Lily said as they unlocked the door.

"Be careful!" Rita called out to them.

The Capitol Regency was four blocks and another world away. The first two blocks were full of barricaded windows and empty store fronts, the next two became gentrified.

At a large intersection they spied the elegant façade of the hotel, its gold and glass doorway bracketed by potted trees, canopies protecting its emerging occupants from the elements.

Lily slowed uncertainly as they approached the entrance, where the liveried doorman guarded the door.

Betty sailed forward serenely.

He looked at them a bit suspiciously, but Betty merely inclined her chin slightly.

The doorman pulled the large door open and ushered them into the lobby.

Lily exhaled when she saw the interior.

"Holy moley!"

Betty merely glanced around and shrugged slightly. "Welcome to Washington, D.C. darling."

The clattered across the polished marble floors, their reflection keeping pace with them. The lobby had a large ell shape to it, with the front desk occupying the area immediately in front of the doors and a seating area off to the right. The ceiling hung some thirty feet above them; the desk was a massive teak wood affair. Plush couches and chairs were grouped in small seating areas. Betty glanced around and headed toward an empty couch closest to the front desk.

She and Lily settled in.

"Now what?" Lily whispered.

"Now we wait, and we watch and listen." Betty pulled a magazine out of her purse.

"You think you could have brought one for me? I'm feeling a bit exposed here!" Lily muttered.

Betty lowered her magazine and fixed Lily with a stare. "Maybe you can find your own?" She tilted her head toward the interior of the hotel.

"I think I will!" Lily hopped up and strolled down the first hallway off the ell.

Betty thumbed through the magazine without really seeing it. Her eyes kept flicking up to the surroundings. Memories of hotels much like this went through her mind. She felt the fabric of her reality starting to shift.

"Focus!" she muttered to herself.

Beside her, three clerks worked the massive desk, one on the left, one in the middle and one on the right. A steady parade of well-to-do patrons streamed in after being disgorged from limousines out front.

Betty looked up as a pair of men walked through the doorway, then did a double take.

She recognized one of them.

She held the magazine up higher in front of her.

They walked to the clerk on the right, the closest one to her. The clerk began to fawn over them.

"Mr. Wagner. Mr. Sutton. Welcome to the Capitol Regency Hotel! It's our pleasure to be accommodating you tonight."

Betty peered over the top edge of her magazine at the pair. The man on the left was overweight bordering on obese. His face was red and sweaty.

But the man on the right was trim and fit, neatly clad in a suit and tie. He moved with an air of self-confidence; a man well used to situations like this.

She had seen him in New Hampshire before she met Ricky Haverill.

Lily reappeared, hands in her pockets, strolling casually along, looking around with unabashed interest.

She reached Betty and started to speak.

"Shh!" Betty hissed.

"Wha..." wisely Lily shut up.

Betty tipped her head toward the two men.

Lily got it.

The clerk was still fawning over them, making the keys up and telling them all the amenities they had access to. Lily sauntered over past them, her eyes on the rack of newspapers that stood just past the desk. The large man glanced at her; the other not at all.

As she perused the selection, she could hear the conversation.

"Here you are Mr. Wagner, Mr. Sutton. This is Suite 717, the biggest penthouse suite we have. There's a private sauna and hot tub in this suite, our Presidential Deluxe room. Here's our menu if you need anything sent up to your suite. There are complimentary drinks in the room, and unlimited encrypted internet. And if there are any...special requests you might have, simply call down here and ask for me, Ricardo." Smiling, he presented them with the keys and his card.

Wagner pocketed both without a glance and turned away from the desk.

Lily pulled a USA today out of the rack and opened it as the two men walked behind her to the elevator.

Neither one looked at her.

She walked back to the couch and sat down next to Betty, who held the magazine up fully blocking her face.

They sat in silence until the two men disappeared into the elevator.

Betty lowered her magazine and looked at Lily.

"Let's get out of here."

As casually as they could manage, they rose and sauntered out of the seating area and back out onto the busy sidewalk. Lily waited a half a block before saying to Betty, "Well? Who was that?"

"That was Buford Wagner."

"And who is he?"

She looked at Lily. "He is possibly the single most important man in Horace Rock's campaign. Officially his title is 'campaign manager' but unofficially he's the one who can make or break a candidate." She walked in silence for a moment.

"So? What does that mean then?"

"That means Horace Rock will be here tonight as well. For whatever reason they are going to carry on with this event without Ricky being here."

"Oh, with any luck he will be here soon enough." Lily replied.

Betty looked at her. "Did you get a good look?"

Lily nodded. "Yup. The ballroom is all the way down and at the back of the hotel. There's a set of elevators, then a bunch of conference rooms. The restaurant is also in the back, on the other side of the ballroom. I don't see any guest rooms on the first floor."

Betty nodded. "No, in a place like this, they will all be upstairs. Nuts. We're going to have to bring him in through the front door then." She fell silent a moment then asked, "Were you able to hear which floor they are on?"

Lily nodded smugly. "I even have the room number." She replied. "717, a penthouse suite."

"Of course." Betty murmured. Her eyes looked distant for a moment. "That's going to be on a keyed floor.

"What does that mean?" Lily asked.

"You have to have a key to a room on that floor to get up there. The elevator won't go up without it."

"Then how the heck are we going to get Ricky up there?" Lily asked.

Betty clutched her bag closer as they neared the two seedy blocks. "I think I know how to do it."

Chapter Thirty-Eight

Rita jumped as the tap on the door rattled through the room.

Lily peered through the peephole.

"She's back."

Doris was perched awkwardly on the edge of one of the beige beds. She wasn't sure, but she thought the covers were distinctly sticky. She shuddered.

Lily opened the door to Betty who swept in clutching several large bags. "Ta da." she said, brandishing them aloft and cocking a hip coquettishly as she did so. "Mission accomplished."

The women clustered around the bed as she dropped the bags onto them. Ricky stared through mirrored sunglasses from across the small room.

He was definitely starting to get ripe, Lily thought, but wisely, kept it to herself.

Rita held up a garment, a shimmering black and silver knee length dress. "Wow!" she exclaimed.

Betty was opening a small white bag and was pulling out an assortment of items.

"I couldn't be sure they would all fit, so I bought larger sizes and these." She dropped boxes of safety pins on the bed.

Lily had pulled out a hot pink sheath and was staring at it in frank mistrust. "How do you wear something like this?" she asked dubiously, turning it around to look at the back.

Betty reached over and took it from her. "Here. That's mine. This is yours."

She tugged out a black and gray sleeveless dress with a sequined bustier jacket.

"Rita," she said, "That dress you're holding is for you. And Doris..." she tugged a shimmery dark blue jacket and knee length dress out of the bag. "This is yours."

Doris took if from her and turned it in all directions. She had to admit one thing: Betty had great taste in clothing.

"You found all of this in the Goodwill?" Lily asked.

Betty was pulling more items out of another bag. "Yup. And here, clutches and jewelry. It's important to fit in at these."

"This had to cost you a fortune!" Rita exclaimed.

Betty sighed, somewhat wistfully. "Not hardly. I used to spend more than this on a single dress. Let's get dressed."

Lily nodded toward Ricky. "What about him?"

Betty held up another bag. "Not to worry. He'll be just as spiffy as we are. And..." she dug into the bag, "I solved the problem of Ricky looking like Ricky."

She tugged out a bouffant brunette wig, combed back in stiff waves. "No one will recognize him now."

The women stared in mute amazement. Lily started laughing. "Oh, holy hell, Betty! He's going to look like a ten-dollar hooker in that!"

"No, he won't!" Betty shot back.

"It is rather... exuberant." Doris said slowly.

Rita took the wig from Betty and spun it around. "I have some scissors in my travel kit. I can probably tame this dead woodchuck down a bit."

Betty sniffed. "Fine. We need to get dressed and we need to dress Ricky too."

"Let's do him first." Lily said.

Twenty minutes later they stood back and looked at their handiwork. "He doesn't look half bad." Lily mused thoughtfully.

Rita brushed an imaginary speck off of his cold dead shoulder. "He looks rather distinguished."

Doris glanced at the window, noting the deepening shadows as the day slid away. "We need to get dressed and get over there."

"Give me the wig first." Rita said.

Chapter Thirty-Nine

It was almost an hour later when Rita cautiously opened the door of the motel and checked both directions. The small lot was quiet.

Cars bustled past on the street and a fair number of pedestrians she noted. She looked back at the women and Ricky and nodded. "Four blocks. We can do this."

They filed out of the room, pushing Ricky ahead of them and turned left toward the Capitol Regency Hotel.

Lily clomped along reaching back to adjust an unseen wedgie. "How do you women walk in these things?" she asked.

Betty snorted. "Please. Those are flats, sensible shoes." She shimmied along balanced on stiletto heels, gliding in her pink sheath.

Doris clutched her bag tightly to her side, feeling oddly glamorous. She glanced down and the shimmering navy blue on her torso. She had to hand it to Betty; she definitely had good taste in clothing.

"So, we all know our roles, right?" Lily hissed as they

drew near the door. Doris nodded tightly as did Rita. Betty smiled, a serene smile.

Lily glanced at her again. "You aren't exactly going to be unnoticeable you know."

"That's the idea." Betty replied demurely.

She gave a dazzling smile at the doorman who swept the door open and gestured them into the lobby with a white gloved hand.

Betty glanced around the space again and headed toward the smaller ell with the fireplace and couch in front of it. No one was occupying it.

They settled in, somewhat gingerly thanks to the safety pins holding everything in place.

Betty and Lily made eye contact. Lily smiled and nodded. She sat back and waited.

People filed into the lobby in twos and threes, heading to the front desk. Lily's eyes lit on an older couple checking in at the right-side clerk.

The clerk in the middle was momentarily free, but more people were coming into the lobby.

She hopped up and headed over toward them.

"Don't stomp!" Betty hissed after her.

She reached the counter ahead of a party of four people, laden with luggage and loudly discussing traffic in the city.

The clerk, a young man, looked up at her with a practiced smile.

"Checking in?"

"Actually, I already did. But I had a question." The clerk's smile held but his eyes took a faint squint.

"I noticed the spa is only open until 10:00 p.m. What happens if I'm still in the spa when it closes?"

The squint became more pronounced. "Then you would have to vacate it for the evening ma'am."

"But what if I'm right in the middle of something, you know? Would I have to stop doing that and leave?"

Beside her the couple was signing the paperwork, and the clerk was making up their keys.

The clerk's smile began to slip. "Like... right in the middle of what?" he asked.

Glancing around conspiratorially, she leaned in. "You know, it's been forever since my husband and I...well...you know. I'm hoping this weekend puts some spring in the old bird's step, or maybe the old bird's pecker."

The couple next to her had collected their keys. The clerk gestured toward the hallway and the elevators. They turned to go.

The clerk was professional. He clamped his lips shut and managed to reply to her in an even tone, even as his face flushed. "Ma'am, while I certainly hope you get some spring in his pecker again, I might remind you that you can't do those sorts of things in the spa area. Please do that in your room."

Lily beamed at him and gave him a thumbs up. "Okay then, well thank you."

She turned and headed toward the hallway the older couple had disappeared into as the noisy group behind her crowded up to the counter.

She reached the elevator just as it opened. The couple entered and pressed the button for the fourth floor. The man looked at her with an eyebrow raised. Lily smiled. "Same, thanks."

She settled in and waited as they rode up.

The door hissed open on the fourth floor. Lily hesitated a moment, letting the couple emerge ahead of her. She followed along some fifteen feet back. He checked their key card and stopped at room 426. He swiped the key across the lock as Lily walked past them, her gaze focused down the hall.

As soon as she heard the door close behind them, she turned and sprinted back to the elevator.

The front desk was crowded now with all three clerks bustling. Lily waited for a few moments and approached the clerk on the left.

"Excuse me. I'm Mrs. Ingallson. We're in room 426 and my husband forgot to get another key card for our daughter."

The clerk glanced up at her and barely registered her. He grabbed another key card and programmed it. "Here you are ma'am."

"Thank you." She replied sweetly and took her leave.

Betty rose and glided graciously across the foyer as Lily walked toward her. She palmed the key card from Lily and headed to the desk.

The middle clerk glanced up as Betty approached him. She placed the card on the counter. "My key card doesn't work." She said haughtily.

"I'm sorry ma'am." He glanced at the card. "What room are you in?"

"717." She sniffed.

He paused, frowning. "Um, I'm sorry, but who is the room registered to?"

Betty fixed him with a frozen glare. "The SUITE is registered to my husband, Buford Wagner." She held her breath.

He glanced at her again as if he was about to say something, then ran his eyes over her. He took the card and slid it into the machine. "Here you go ma'am. I'm sorry; it's just that we have to be careful on the penthouse floor."

Imperiously, she swept the card off the counter and

turned away. "You have to keep the riff-raff out. I understand."

She glided across the lobby toward the elevator without looking toward Doris, Rita Lily and Ricky.

They waited four agonizingly long minutes then stood up and casually strolled toward the elevator. Lily pushed Ricky along, who sported a rather distinct mullet and a thin mustache now. Doris walked as regally as her stiff body allowed. They entered the elevator and pressed the button for floor number 5.

Betty was in front of the window in the hallway overlooking the lot when the doors opened. She turned and hustled into the lift.

"Okay girls. Showtime." Lily said brightly.

Doris hugged her bag and Rita looked at her with worried eyes.

"I still don't like this. Rita murmured.

"Too late now." Lily replied,

They inserted the key card into the slot and the light for the seventh floor lit up.

"Well, it works so far." Doris muttered.

"It will work." Betty said. "Remember; when we get off, we go right and go around the corner. Rita goes left to 717. Rita, if anyone answers the door, tell them you are with the seating committee, and that they want to talk to them about last minute changes in the arrangements. Tell them they're needed downstairs. If no one answers, we're golden."

Rita swallowed noisily.

The lift doors slid open revealing a hallway clad in shades of red and gold, far posher than the lower floors. Candelabras lit the way with pools of soft light.

Ricky thumped over the edge of the elevator into the hall and the women followed.

Rita took a deep breath and turned away from them. The door to 717 was the only one on the wall on the right side.

She rapped sharply on the door.

There was no sound.

She rapped again, harder.

Still nothing.

Doris, Lily and Betty peered around the corner.

Gulping, Rita nodded at them. They quickly scurried around the corner and hustled to the room.

With a silent prayer, Rita swiped the keypad with the card.

Nothing.

She swiped again. A red light glowed.

"Damn it all!" she hissed.

"Here! Give it to me." Betty said as the elevator chimed behind them.

She tapped the card swiftly. The light glowed green, and the door opened.

"Quickly!" Betty whispered. They rammed Ricky through the doorway and pushed their way into the room in a jumble.

The elevator doors sighed open as their door clicked shut.

They froze holding their breaths.

Faint voices in the hallway faded as the guests made their way toward a distant room.

They exhaled shaky breaths.

Doris closed her eyes momentarily as black spots danced. Opening them again, she looked around at their surroundings.

They were in a large foyer, with a small table under a mirror. Fresh flowers adorned it, real ones. The wallpaper was patterned gold, the carpeting shades of gold and red. A small antechamber for putting coats or luggage in was located off of the right-side wall. A doorway leading into the suite proper was straight ahead.

Looking through the entrance, she saw a large room lavishly furnished. Her curiosity overwhelmed her fear for a moment, and she stepped forward to look into it.

The suite was the size of three large hotel rooms, complete with a bar and a seating area with two sofas and two armchairs. An fully equipped office area occupied one corner. Three doors led off of the central room; one to a bathroom, the other two to large bedrooms.

Lily stepped past her into the room. "Geeze Louise," she said. "We were in the wrong business. We should have gone into politics."

Betty rolled Ricky into the living room and glanced around, faintly wistful.

"Jon and I had rooms like this. Well almost like this, just a bit smaller."

Rita was peeking into the bathroom. "There's a jacuzzi tub, a shower and a sauna!" she exclaimed.

Doris looked around as her discomfort returned. "Okay, enough. We did it. Now let's get out of here!"

"Where should we put him?" Rita asked.

"Just leave him in the wheelchair. Let's go!" Doris sputtered.

She didn't want to be in this room another second.

"Now wait a minute here." Lily said. "Let's put him in one of the chairs so we can take ours."

"What? Why?" Doris's voice rose.

"Because it cost me a bunch of money is why. I can return it and get it refunded. I saved all the labels." Lily told her.

"Just leave it!"

"No! Come on now, it won't take but a second. And then you can use it if your hip gets too bad."

"She has a good point you know." Betty said. "You're walking mighty stiff today."

"Let's just do it quick and get out of here!" Rita grabbed one of Ricky's arms as she said that.

"Oh, for Pete's sake! Hurry up then!" Doris swore she was going to kill them all when... if... they got home.

Lily and Rita lifted Ricky as Betty pulled the chair out from under him. They seated him in the armchair on the right side.

"Wait." Lily leaned over and rotated one leg up, crossing his ankle over the opposite knee. "There. He looks rights as rain now."

"Can we please get OUT of here?" Doris hissed.

"Yeah, yeah. Let's go."

They spun the chair around toward the hallway... and froze.

"Not so fast ladies." said Buford Wagner.

Chapter Forty

"Jim, you can't keep driving around the block!"

"I've been looking for a place to park where we won't get towed!" Jim's face was flushed red. "I wish I had my cruiser. I could park it anywhere."

"A Vermont cruiser? Not hardly, Jim." Jorge replied dryly.

"Just drop us off at the curb then and find someplace. We'll catch up to you." Sandy told him.

Jim scowled. "I ain't really liking the thought of you going off on your own here!"

"We're going to lose them!" Sandy closed her eyes in frustration.

They had circled the area around the hotel multiple times when their attention was caught by a splash of bright pink. A cluster of older women dressed in fancy clothing pushing a wheelchair had caught their eye.

"There they are!" Jorge had shouted.

And then Washington traffic had worked its magic on them. So close they could see them, they were brought to a halt time and time again. The bright pink splash became smaller and smaller on the sidewalk before turning into and disappearing into the Capitol Regency Hotel.

Jim turned down a side street. Cars lined both sides, bumper to bumper.

Jorge leaned forward. "Jim, I'll look out for her. Drop us off. You go back down the street we saw them on. There has to be someplace they came from, and it can't be far. Maybe there's a parking lot."

Jim glanced at Sandy; uncertainty written in his face.

"I'll keep an eye on her." Jorge promised.

"Hey!" Sandy's eyes narrowed dangerously.

Jorge caught her eye and shook his head.

With a muttered curse, Jim swung back around the block onto the road in front of the hotel. Limousines were lined up disgorging passengers. He stopped for a traffic light.

Sandy popped her door open. "This is good. Come as soon as you can!"

She leapt out into the road and ran up onto the sidewalk.

With a shrug to Jim, Jorge followed her.

Sandy charged ahead of Jorge to the front door of the hotel...where the doorman promptly stopped her.

"May I ask your business please?" he said icily, eyeing her outfit.

"My business is none of YOUR business!" she retorted, trying to push through the doorway.

He blocked her path.

"I don't believe you have the right place ma'am." The doorman replied.

Jorge reached her then and pulled a card out of his pocket. "I'm Jorge Maxim and this is Sandy Case. We're correspondents." He handed the card to the doorman.

He read the card and sniffed, then looked Sandy up and down again, eyeing her sneakers and stained polo shirt. "I'm sorry," he said to Jorge, "But with her dressed like that I must request you use the service entrance in the back." He indicated the sidewalk to the left.

"Are you kidding me?" Jorge sputtered.

The doorman tipped his hat to a couple resplendent in shiny fabric and dripping with jewels.

"We have an important event here tonight. Please go around to the security booth in the rear and tell them your business. If they decide it's okay, you will be issued visitor passes."

He turned away to the next couple, studiously ignoring them.

Sandy's face was dangerously red. "Are you freaking KIDDING me?" she sputtered. "We're the PRESS!"

Jorge was putting his card in his wallet, his face grim. "Welcome to the new Washington D.C., Case. Being the 'press' isn't always respected here now."

"Jorge! We're losing them every second we spend out here!"

"I know, I know!" He grabbed her arm and pulled her away from the front door as another limousine pulled up.

"Come on. Let's see what the back is like." They walked down the sidewalk and turned the corner.

This side of the hotel was bustling, but with different activity. Vans, delivery trucks and cars pulled in and out of the gated lot in the back. A booth sat next to the gate, where they could see an obese guard raising the gate for each car.

Several black Government type cars were in the lot as well. Jorge swore softly.

"This isn't going to be easy Case." He told her.

They leaned against the wall of the hotel and watched

the traffic in and out of the lot. The line of cars and trucks into the hotel grew steadily alongside the alleyway they were on. Several vans were parked on the sidewalks outside the lot, their occupants pulling out items and carrying them in instead of trying to get into the lot.

Sandy's eye fell on a white van parked some thirty feet away from them. The uniformed workers were pulling bags of laundry out and carrying them to the gate. The guard was letting them in without a second look.

"Jorge!" she hissed. "Come on!"

"Case...what? What are you doing?" Jorge said alarmed as Sandy hustled toward the van.

"Getting in is what I'm doing!" She reached the open side door and grabbed two large plastic bags of soft materials. She thrust one at Jorge. "Take this!"

His eyes had narrowed. He grabbed her arm. "Close, but they won't let us in."

"Why not?" she hissed.

He waved his hand down his body indicating their clothing. "We don't look the part."

"Damn it all!" Sandy sputtered.

Jorge smiled. "Relax. All we need are these." He reached in and grabbed another bag.

Sandy's brow furrowed as she looked in. The bag held white kitchen worker clothes.

Jorge nodded toward the bag she held. "Put that back. This and this are what we need." He plucked another bag out of the van.

Five minutes later the van pulled away from the curb. Jorge and Sandy cautiously emerged from the doorway they'd been huddled in.

Sandy tugged vainly on the baggy white pants she wore, smoothing the white twin buttoned coat.

Jorge rolled his neck and adjusted his white coat; his clothing fit better than hers.

He looked at her. "Ready?"

She looked down at herself. "This is ridiculous, you know that."

Jorge smiled. "Act like you belong." They shouldered the two bags they had kept and trudged to the gate.

The fat guard was checking in another delivery truck. He glanced at them and frowned.

Jorge smiled and spoke in heavily accented English. "De boss, he sent us to get de linens for tonight."

"Brinknell's was just here! Why didn't he have them bring them in?"

"Dey bring de wrong ones so de bossman he send us to chase dem and get de right ones." Jorge nodded; his posture obsequious.

The guard rolled his eyes. "Fine." He reached for the gate, then looked at the two of them. "I haven't seen you two before." He said.

Sandy glanced at Jorge and said, "We just got hired yesterday for this event." She yawned. "They didn't tell me it meant being here at the ass crack of dawn until after I signed."

The guard snorted. "Welcome to the Capitol Regency Hotel." He said and raised the gate.

They entered the lot.

Chapter Forty-One

Jim pounded the steering wheel in frustration. Around him, traffic had snarled to a standstill as the motorcade bringing the current President of the United States made its way to the Capitol Regency Hotel.

The outgoing President, George Montbalm had served his eight years, aging noticeably before the cameras he faced daily. Now he was on his way to endorse Horace Rock as his potential successor, sending a wave of closed streets and traffic nightmares ahead of him.

Jim had tried to make one more swing around the hotel in a vain attempt to find something...anything...where he could leave the car. It was one swing too many.

Now he wished he had simply abandoned it when Sandy and Jorge had bailed out.

Horns blared and drivers shouted epitaphs at one another as he drummed his fingers impatiently on the wheel.

Sandy was going to get herself in trouble again.

He knew it.

He looked around at the busy sidewalks, the scooters weaving in and out of the standstill traffic. The hotel was behind him some four blocks back now.

She was going to get herself in trouble again. He just knew it!

Impatiently, he drummed his fingers on the wheel as car horns rose in a cacophony around him. Gol durned fools; always thinking making noise was going to magically open up a blocked road.

He looked in his side mirror. He could just see the edge of the roof on the hotel Sandy had gone tearing into.

That woman! She was going to be the death of him yet. His life had been serene before she came along.

Well serene and boring, he had to admit.

Brownville was a great place to grow up and live, but if you weren't hooked up by age 25, there just weren't many options left for a man like him. And when he was younger, he'd been so focused, first on running the family farm and then on becoming an officer of the law, that he simply hadn't realized time was slipping away like that.

Hadn't truly realized it until the day Sandy blew into town like a derecho. He smiled briefly at the memory.

Oh she drove him crazy sometimes, but he always preferred the crazy to not having her in his life. Still, when you were hard-wired to take care of those you loved, the way she would kite off into danger was maddening at times.

More than once he had told himself he was done, only to change his mind three minutes later.

He eyed the hotel again. He had a bad feeling about this.

The horns bleated endlessly around him. They weren't gonna move anytime soon, that was for sure.

With a muttered curse, he flung open the door of the car

and started trotting back up the road weaving between stopped cars, his eyes set on the distant buildings that surrounded the Capitol Regency Hotel.

Chapter Forty-Two

Buford Wagner was a trim 57-year-old. His pinstriped suit was meticulous, his gray goatee and mustache trimmed closely. Brown eyes flickered from face to face, then settled on Ricky. He frowned.

"You want to enlighten me as to why you ladies and gentleman are in my suite? The clerk told me my 'wife' just came down for a new key; said hers wasn't working." He raked his eyes up and down Betty. "As you may realize, being that my wife isn't with me on this trip, you can imagine my curiosity." He looked again at Ricky, his gaze frankly suspicious.

"Who are you people?" he touched his lapel. "You have thirty seconds to fill me in before I call the Secret Service in. They happen to be outside my door right now."

Doris's legs shook. She felt her knees start to buckle. Lily saw it and grabbed her guiding her into the wheelchair where she landed with a thump.

"Ah shit." Lily said.

They exchanged glances.

"You have twenty seconds left." Buford said.

Betty sighed and stepped forward. "Okay. Alright. This was all my fault. But he had responsibility for it too!" She pointed at Ricky.

"Who IS that?" Buford asked, his gaze narrowing.

"Ricky Haverill." Lily said in a resigned tone.

"WHAT?" Bufords head snapped back at him. "Where's he been? We looked everywhere for him!" He strode over to him and grabbed his upper arm then recoiled.

"Wha... what's wrong with him? Why is he so stiff?"

"Because he is one." Lily said sadly.

"He's WHAT?" Buford shook his arm. "Is he dead?"

"He is, but he went out with a bang if that's any consolation." Betty said.

Buford whirled to face them, his jaw hanging.

He looked back and forth between Ricky and the women. His face regained composure.

He folded his arms and faced them.

"Sit down. Now!"

Rita and Lily edged over to the couch and perched on it. Betty sighed and gracefully folded herself into the empty armchair. Doris stayed in the wheelchair, defeated.

"Tell me exactly what happened that caused Richard Haverill's death and why he is sitting here in this get up."

"Well," Betty began, "I was over to the Legion Hall for Sunday night drinks when he came into the bar. We hit it off, and he ended up coming home with me. I didn't know who he was."

Buford closed his eyes momentarily. "Great. Just great. Okay what happened then?"

"Well what do you think happened?" Lily interjected. "They started going at it like rabid raccoons. None of us got a wink of sleep for hours!"

Buford's left eye twitched. "How did he end up dead?"

"Well one minute he was going for the gold, and I was just about to have the big O when he suddenly made this weird grunting noise, then he groaned and collapsed on me. And he wouldn't move!" Tears sprang into Betty's eyes. "I thought he was going to kill me!"

Buford looked at Ricky with a scowl. "Damn horndog never could keep his dick in his pants. Why is he so weird looking? Is he embalmed?"

"Oh, no." Lily said brightly. "He's taxidermized."

Buford Wagner was a man who ruled corporate boardrooms. His poker face had no comparison.

It deserted him now.

"He's WHAT?" he shouted.

"Taxidermized." Lily said again.

"Why the HELL did you do that?"

"Because he was going to start stinking and we couldn't get enough ice. So my nephew took care of that. Put a slick frame in him too."

"Well maybe he wasn't quite as good at it as you think Lily." Rita said.

"And why is that?" Buford asked.

"He didn't have human eyes, so he had to make do with bear eyes. That's why he's wearing those spiffy shades." Lily replied.

Buford gave them a hard look then lifted the glasses. He jumped back when he saw the glaring brown bear eyes.

"Jesus H. Christ!" he said.

Betty frowned and turned to Lily. "Why do people always say that? What is Jesus's middle name? Hector? Horace? Harold?"

"Quiet!" Buford barked.

He folded his arms and placed his right hand over his mouth contemplatively. He stared at Ricky for a long moment then reached out and rotated his left arm out, then in, noting how it turned and clicked. "How did he do this? You said it was your nephew?" He stared hard at Lily.

She nodded hesitantly.

"What's his name?"

She swallowed noisily and looked around at the others. They stared back mutely.

"Um. Hiram."

"Hiram what?"

"Wa...Waller. Hiram Waller. Look, he didn't do anything wrong. I asked him to do this for me. He's a good boy, and he's clever. Look at the spiffy frame he made! He engineered that. Ricky moves almost as if he were still alive."

"Who else was involved in this?" Buford gave them a piercing stare.

They all exchanged looks.

"No...no one." Betty said.

"When we realized who he was, all we wanted to do was get him back to the campaign bus. But it had left New Hampshire." Doris said. "And this was the next stop. So we decided to bring him here and just kind of drop him off someplace."

"And why didn't you call the police?" Buford pinned her with a glare.

Doris wilted under his scrutiny. "I didn't want anything to happen to us. To happen to Betty. She's had kind of a... tough time of late." She gazed at Betty sadly as tears filled her eyes. She looked back at Buford beseechingly. "I didn't want us to get dragged through the press. I wanted our life to go on the way it always had, except maybe we were going to have to have a conversation with Betty about her behavior."

Betty's head snapped around. "Me? Me? What's wrong with me?"

The women exchanged sad glances. Buford's eyes narrowed. He turned back to Ricky Haverill and cast a critical eye over him. "He looks like he's lost some weight."

Lily looked down and shifted uncomfortably. "Well that's because I only gave Hiram forty-eight hours to do this. Normally it takes months if not years to do this kind of work."

Lily leaned closer to Ricky and wrinkled her nose. "He might not have completely cured him either. He smells like an old cellar hole."

"And he looks like something you see in a funhouse mirror." Buford replied tartly.

Lily opened her mouth to reply but Buford raised his hand, cutting her off. "Enough."

They fell into an uneasy silence. Buford tugged his lapel up slightly to his mouth and muttered something into it.

They heard the doorway to the hall open.

Two Secret Service men glided into the room, all sunglasses and dark suits. Buford waved his hand at the women. "Search them, but you can leave him."

Doris sighed and handed over her handbag mutely, as did Lily and Rita.

Betty pulled her closer and tried to shield it from them.

They responded with alacrity.

"Ow! Hey you didn't have to be rude!" she yelped as they wrenched her bag out from under her arm.

The taller of the two agents upended her purse on the coffee table. Frankie fell out and landed with a squishy thud on the polished wood.

Secret Service agents are trained in all manner of

threats. They know how to identify and neutralize threats instantly, how to maintain a deadpan expression and how to pretend to not notice or react to sensitive moments around their charges.

Frankie didn't fall into any of those situations.

The taller dark-haired agent gaped noticeably before regaining his composure. The shorter sandy-haired one looked closer, then recoiled slightly. A small smirk flitted across his mouth.

"What the hell is THAT?" For the second time that day, Buford was left speechless.

"Is that a dildo?"

"That's Frankie." Betty offered demurely.

Buford leaned slightly closer, his nose wrinkling. "Why is that thing in your purse?"

"Frankie goes everyplace with me." Betty said. She crossed her ankle coquettishly and reached up to fluff her hair. "You never know when you might need a good orga..."

"I think he's heard enough, Betty!" Doris cut her off.

The shorter Secret Service agent stifled a grin.

Buford closed his eyes for a moment and massaged the bridge of his nose. Opening them again, he glared at them. "You ladies stay right here with him." He indicated the shorter agent.

"You, outside." He tilted his head toward the other agent.

They left the room.

"I have to pee." Lily whispered.

"Hold it!" hissed Rita.

It felt like days, but it was probably only a half an hour before there was noise in the hallway. There was a low mutter in the foyer, then a man entered the room with Buford half a step behind him.

Doris, Rita, Lily and Betty looked at him and gasped.

Horace Rock was a commanding presence on television but in person he was a force to be reckoned with. The leading candidate for the position of President of the United States, he had been enjoying a comfortable lead in the polls in the recent months leading up to the election.

He stopped and took a long look at Ricky Haverill, then he looked from woman to woman, making eye contact with each of them.

Doris felt her breath stop in her chest.

"Good afternoon, ladies." His voice was low and warm, surprisingly friendly. "I understand you brought Richard back to us."

Doris flushed as Betty preened visibly.

"Oh Mr. Rock! What an honor and a privilege it is to meet you, sir!"

"The pleasure is all mine, Ms. O'Donnell, although we do seem to have ourselves a rather sticky situation on our hands now thanks to your peccadillos with Mr. Haverill, and with those numerous other gentlemen over the past year."

Doris, Lily and Rita exchanged alarmed looks.

"Um, Mr. Almost-President, how, um did you know about that?" Lily stammered.

Horace Rock looked at her with a warm smile that came nowhere near his eyes. "Why my dears, I know all about you, each of you. I know your names. I know where you live, what you drive, what you like to eat for dinner. I know everything about you now, trust me."

Lily gulped audibly.

Horace turned back to Ricky and stared at him with a calculating look for a long moment. Then the wolf smile returned to his face, and he turned to the women again. "If you'll excuse me, I have to have a word with Mr. Wagner here. Stay right where you are."

The threat was concealed in a velvet glove, but it was there.

The men left the room.

Chapter Forty-Three

Horace Rock and Buford Wagner entered the master bedroom. Buford slid the door shut behind them, blocking them from the women who sat in abject despair.

Horace rubbed his face. "I've been in politics going on forty years now, and I have to say, I have never, EVER had anyone on my staff or in my office returned to me dead and stuffed. And that included that stint as an ambassador to Saudi Arabia!" Horace's face took on a pink cast. "What the HELL were those old ladies thinking?"

Buford shook his head. "Mr. Rock, I know this is distressing, but I have a damage control plan in place. We can tell everyone he was killed in a car wreck up north, ended up in a pond so we didn't find him right away. Or maybe a good car fire. You can still get Rory Sathers as your running mate. I think the sympathy vote alone will swing the states we aren't strongest in yet. We can salvage this."

Horace was already shaking his head. "I didn't choose that pea brain Sathers for a reason. No, no actually I think those old women might have done us a favor."

Buford's brow furrowed. "A favor? They killed your VP and STUFFED him for Christ's sake! How is THAT a FAVOR?"

Horace walked over to the bar that was positioned in the corner and poured himself a finger of neat whiskey. He smiled serenely. "You have to admit, Haverill was a dumb son of a bitch. We were constantly baby-sitting him. Nothing could come out of his mouth unless it was scripted. He was always going off with anything strange that would let him under their skirt. Now, well now he's controllable."

Buford gaped at him. "He's controllable? He's dead is what he is! I guess that's the ultimate control, but it's hardly what you want in your running mate."

He tossed back his drink. "On the contrary." Horace replied. "He's a better candidate now than he was when he was alive."

Buford's eyes narrowed.

Horace rubbed his chin for a moment, his eyes calculating.

"You said these women were alone?"

Buford nodded. "They have little to no family, except for one nephew and one daughter that rough one has. They share a house in Brownville, a small town in Vermont. The house acts as a de facto rest home for a few women. The fat one in the wheelchair owns it."

Horace replied, "And Betty, the one in pink Haverill was screwing, she's losing her marbles, isn't she?"

Buford nodded. "The reports indicated she's been having a lot of one-night stands recently."

Horace grimaced slightly.

They fell silent for a moment. Horace looked at his watch. "Time to get downstairs, Buford." He locked eyes with him. "Take care of them."

"You're sure of that sir?"

"As sure as I have ever been. Oh, and get that penis off my damn coffee table and have it sanitized too."

"As you wish, sir."

Chapter Forty-Four

Sandy and Jorge moved along with the stream of workers heading into the back doorway of the hotel. Jorge muttered a curse; they were swiping key cards to open the door.

"Damn it all!" Sandy blurted.

Ahead of them a young Latin woman strode briskly toward the door. She had the harried air of a mother, her hair already escaping her carefully pulled up bun. She held an oversized bag, which she now dug through frantically.

She wore a blue maid's uniform.

Jorge sprinted forward as she pulled her key card out. "Hola!" he called out, "Por favor, Podemos entrar?" he indicated the bags they held. "El jefe nos envio a buscarlos y olvidamos los neustros."

She shrugged and held the door, "Si, date prisa."

"Gracias." Jorge said smiling warmly at her. "Eres tan amable como eres hermosa."

She flushed and smiled shyly at him. He gave her a smile and a wink.

She held the door open, and they followed her inside.

They slowed their steps as she hurried down the long utilitarian hallway. They could hear the bustle and noise of the kitchen. Jorge grabbed Sandy's arm and tugged her into a side hallway that connected with the main one. He whispered to her, "We can't be seen. Come on. Let's find a room where we can get rid of these." He tugged his coat.

"Oh I don't know." Sandy replied acerbically. "I think that look suits you. That young woman seemed to like you just fine wearing that."

"Shut up, Case. Maybe one day you'll understand about getting further by using honey instead of vinegar." Jorge stopped and looked into a small room on the left. Serving carts and trays were stacked in here, along with stacks of table linens.

"Here!" He ducked in and tossed the bag in the corner then started yanking his coat off. Sandy followed suit.

Jorge smoothed a hand over his shirt and adjusted his collar. He eyed Sandy. "You still look like an unmade bed."

"Well excuse me for not having time to change before we flew out of town."

He shook his head. "Hopefully no one will eject you."

Sandy looked down at herself. "Jorge, if they do, don't you DARE let those ladies get away."

"Oh, I promise you, I won't." He looked cautiously out the door, leaning back in as two people crossed the intersection of the hallways they had just come from. "Come on."

They headed out and away from the kitchen area. "Where do we go?" Sandy asked.

"This has to be the back service entrance to the conference and ballrooms." Jorge said. "Most hotels have the two entrances, one for staff and one for guests."

They came to a pair of swinging doors.

"Let's see if this is it." Sandy started to push them open.

Jorge grabbed her hand. He shook his head. "No. We look first." He nodded toward a small window next to it.

"Why is this here?" Sandy asked.

"It's likely a one-way mirror." Jorge told her. "They'd use it to judge when it was time to enter with the next round."

She peered through the window. "Holy shit!" Sandy exclaimed. Jorge pushed in next to her.

The window looked into an opulent ballroom. Brilliant gold chandeliers hung over every area; huge pedestals filled with flowers and round tables with gold-colored silverware and sparkling china dotted the room.

There were also agents stationed around the room in black suits looking for all the world like bats at a wedding.

"Not here." Jorge said and drew Sandy down the hallway.

"That was the longest route to the front desk I have ever taken!" Sandy muttered ten minutes later as she and Jorge drifted through the lobby in a group of chattering people.

Outside they could see the doorman's broad blue coated back as he guarded his kingdom.

"Now what?" Sandy muttered.

Jorge's eyes were roaming around the room.

He looked at her. "Wait over there." He indicated the area of sofas near the fireplace where a dozen people sat chatting.

"Why can't I stay with you?" Sandy grumbled.

"Because you look like a cleaning lady. Now just trust me, this is my territory, okay?"

Jorge squared his shoulders up and watched the clerks. They were steadily busy with momentary breaks. The one on the left had a lull. Jorge strode over to him. "Excuse me.

I'm looking for a tall blonde woman in a hot pink dress. Have you seen her?" The clerk glanced up at him with a furrowed brow. "I'm sorry sir, but what is your business?" Jorge drew his business card out of his wallet. "I'm with the Washington Daily News, and I am supposed to be finding her to set up my interview with Horace Rock tonight." The middle clerk glanced over and said, "Oh, that's Buford Wagner's wife. She was here just a little while ago."

"Oh, right. My editor just told me to go find 'the blonde woman' in charge of Rock's publicity schedule. Maybe he should have mentioned her relationship to Wagner to me." Jorge replied dryly.

The clerk smiled. "Bosses are the same no matter where you work, huh?"

"You aren't kidding." Jorge shook his head as he slid his card back into his wallet. "Any idea where she went?"

The clerk shrugged. "She was headed up to their suite last I saw."

"Okay, I'll try calling her then. Thank you." Jorge pulled his phone out and turned away from the desk.

He rejoined Sandy on the couch.

"She told them she was Buford Wagner's wife, Horace Rocks' right-hand man."

Sandy's eyes had widened. "I know who he is. She told them she was his WIFE?"

Jorge nodded. "They aren't here involuntarily. Whatever is going on, they're in it up to their wrinkled necks."

Sandy looked past him and spied Jim on the sidewalk. He was being detained by the doorman.

Jorge saw her staring and looked over his shoulder. "Hey, I should go help him get in."

Sandy grabbed his arm and shook her head. "No!"

"No?"

"No. He thinks they are innocent. He'll never let us get the story. No, we have to leave him outside."

"Case. He's your boyfriend!" Jorge hissed.

"All the more reason I can't have him in the middle." She jumped up and grabbed Jorge's arm. "Come on! Let's go upstairs before he sees us!" She hauled him around the corner toward the elevator.

The door thumped open, disgorging four people. Sandy and Jorge crowded in. She jabbed the door close button impatiently, closing the doors. "Where do you think they are?" Sandy asked as the elevator began to rise. Jorge was looking at the panel.

"The seventh floor." He said in a resigned tone.

"How do you know that?" Sandy asked.

Jorge gestured to the panel. "Because it's the one floor we aren't going to be able to access."

She saw the key card slot.

"Shit!" she muttered.

"Yup." Jorge replied.

"So now what?"

Jorge looked her up and down. "Now we find some way to camouflage you and we wait downstairs until they appear."

Sandy turned and glared at him. "Like hell we do, Maxim. We didn't go through all of this to sit around in a hotel lobby."

Jorge's eyes narrowed. "Uh oh. I know THAT look. What are you thinking?"

Sandy smiled. "Come with me."

Chapter Forty-Five

Sandy stabbed the down button on the elevator impatiently.

Jorge eyed her narrowly. "You mind telling me what you have in mind here, Case?"

The doors sighed shut, and the elevator began to glide downward.

"Clearly their security is ramped up today because of the gala. And almost certainly the ladies are upstairs, most likely in Buford Wagner's suite. So desperate times call for desperate measures."

"Why am I not liking the sound of this?" Jorge lamented.

Sandy smiled sweetly.

The elevator jounced gently to a halt on the ground floor. The rear doors slid open.

Jorge's glanced into the plain hallway then back at her.

"The service area?" he asked.

Sandy was already exiting the elevator, her bag bouncing off the small of her back.

"Yup." Was all she said.

"Case..." Jorge said warningly.

She waved him off and headed down the hallway at a speed walk. Jorge hustled to keep up.

"You're reminding me WHY I chose to leave Brownville in the first place!" Jorge sputtered. "I seem to recall many instances where you put my life and limb at risk!"

"And helped you get that Pulitzer." Sandy retorted as she slowed to poke her head into a side room. "Nope." she muttered and kept going. Same with the next two rooms, then, "Here. This one."

Jorge followed her into what looked like the changing room of a gym. Rows of lockers lined the three walls, with two free standing rows in the middle. No one was in the room.

"Case!" Jorge hissed, "What the hell are you up to?"

She shook her head to silence him as her eyes scanned the rows of lockers. Some sported combination locks or keyed locks brought in by the owners.

But others did not.

She glanced around the room. "Jorge, watch the door. If you see anyone coming, let me know."

"I do NOT like the sound of this."

"But you liked the sound of the audience applauding at that Pulitzer ceremony, didn't you?"

"Jesus." Jorge muttered, but he went to stand in the door where he could peer down the hallway.

Sandy started opening the unlocked lockers. The first five were empty. But then, the sixth one wasn't. She tugged out a doorman's uniform and frowned at it. "Nuts." She tossed it on one of the rows of benches.

The seventh, eighth and ninth lockers were empty. The tenth however made Sandy smile, a feral one.

"Got it!" she hissed.

"Got what?" Jorge turned back.

"What we need." She held up the housekeeping uniform and waved the flat key card at him.

Jorge's brow wrinkled. "You think that can get us in?"

"This is our key to everywhere, Jorge."

He looked her up and down. "Not looking like that it is." He nodded at the uniform. "Will that fit you?"

She spun it around. "It's made for an overweight hippo, so yes, it will fit. Just not well."

"This isn't a beauty contest, Case." Jorge stepped back into the room and picked up the doorman's outfit. "I can fit into this one."

Sandy beamed at him. "Let's do it."

Five minutes later, they peered around the corner warily.

The hallway remained empty. Distant clatter and voices marked the kitchen to the left. The elevator was back to the right.

"Ready?" Jorge whispered.

Sandy nodded then smirked as she looked at him. "God, I want a photo of this when we get a moment."

The uniform had been made for a man several inches taller and about 50 pounds heavier than Jorge. The cuffs on the dual striped legs puddled around his ankles; the coat hung limply. Gold braid adorned his shoulders, a blue hat with a shiny black brim crowned his head and he sported a pair of white gloves.

He scowled at her. "The same can be said for you, you know."

Sandy's blue and white housekeeping uniform was made of shapeless, scratchy polyester. There was a white apron that covered her chest and cinched around her waist. She had used it to bind the layers of extra fabric the uniform was leaving on her. The rest of it still bubbled out in various places, designed to be worn by someone many pounds heavier.

She had tamed her unruly hair into a messy bun. The key lanyard hung around her neck.

Her oversized bag hung off one shoulder, a jarring note to her outfit. Jorge frowned at it.

Sandy glanced over her shoulder. "I know. There's a cart in the third room. I can stash it underneath the towels and use the cart as a prop."

She looked up at him and smiled wolfishly.

"Let's roll, Maxim."

Chapter Forty-Six

The elevator doors opened smoothly. Sandy and Jorge crowded into it, Sandy pushing a housekeeping cart that now contained her bag. She inserted her key card into the keyed floor slot.

It remained stubbornly dark.

She tried again.

Nothing.

"Damn it all!" she said.

Jorge placed a hand on her arm. "We may have to be up above the basement for that to work. Let's start with the sixth floor instead." He pressed the button.

The floor light lit up.

The elevator jerked upward with a creak and started up. It stopped at the first floor, the lobby floor. The door opened and two men entered the elevator. They wore dark suits and annoyed expressions.

Jorge felt Sandy stiffen.

The spared only a contemptuous look at the two of them before stabbing the button for the seventh floor.

It refused to light up.

"Damn it!" Said the tall skinny guy with the sloping forehead. His partner, a short swarthy man wore a scowl etched into his features.

"I thought you said we had access?" hissed the skinny one.

The short man was stabbing at the buttons on the elevator. "That's what the Boss just told me."

"Clearly the Boss didn't tell you everything." remarked the skinny man acerbically.

Sandy stood stiffly, staring at the elevator lights. She reached over and pressed one of the buttons. Jorge glanced at her puzzled but said nothing.

The door rolled open at the fourth floor and Sandy almost bolted through, turning her head to avoid eye contact. Jorge followed her out.

The doors closed.

"What the hell was that about, Case?"

She jerked her head toward the elevator that had closed. "Those happened to be the two feds we were TRACKING Jorge!"

"Oh!"

"Yeah, 'oh' is right!" she snapped.

"Well let's go down the hallway and take the other elevat..." Jorge started to say as the doors opened again.

The two feds, Curtis Danville and Harold Noth glared at them from the interior of the lift.

"You!" Curtis barked. "We need you! Federal business!"

Sandy started to back away, moving the cart between her and the feds. "Wha.. wha?"

"Are you stupid? You're now under the order of the United States of America! Get back into this elevator!"

Jorge grabbed her upper arm and smiled at them.

"Pardon her gentleman. No hablo Ingles." He gripped her upper arm in a death grip.

Beside him Sandy was mute in astonishment. Jorge met her eyes and shook his head microscopically.

Sandy pursed her lips and replied in a low voice, "Comer mierda."

Jorge's eyes bulged as he heard her telling the feds to consume feces. His grip on her arm tightened.

Mercifully neither one understood Spanish.

The short one gestured into the elevator. "Get in then. We have important business, and we need her."

She started to push the cart back into the elevator.

"Leave that!" the tall skinny one, who was Harold Noth barked. He shoved the cart, which had Sandy's omnipresent bag concealed in it, to the side.

"Just you two!"

Jorge eyed the two men, noting the shoulder holsters and the strained, pissed off expressions. He guided Sandy into the elevator.

With a beseeching glance at the abandoned cart, she allowed herself to be pushed into the elevator. The doors closed.

"You." Curtis directed at Sandy. "Get us into the seventh floor." He nodded toward the key card slot.

Sandy glanced at Jorge. He reached down and took the card hanging on the lanyard and inserted it into the slot.

The light for the seventh floor lit up.

"There you go, gentlemen." Jorge said as the doors opened onto the plush red and gold hallway. "We will be on our way now."

"Oh no you don't." said Harold. "We aren't done with her yet. We need access into that room."

He gestured toward the gleaming door to Suite 717.

Sandy clutched the key card to her chest. "Vete a la mierda." She replied, inviting the men to have intimate relations with themselves.

Jorge's eyes bulged. He reached up and took her upper arm and gave a warning squeeze.

"She's worried about losing her job." Jorge said smoothly.

The short swarthy fed, Curtis was frowning. "Hey, I don't think that's what she said..."

"Trust me, that's what she said. Okay, do what the man asked you to do, er, haz lo que el hombre te pidio." He gave her a warning glare.

Sandy glanced at the feds and back at Jorge. Wisely she decided to keep her mouth shut. With shaking hands, she took the key card and swiped it over the lock.

It glowed green.

The door to the suite burst open and two dark-suited men with ear buds emerged. They moved to either side of the doorway in a fluid motion.

Both held guns on the four of them.

"Hey!" Harold yelped. "You can't do that! We're the CIA!"

"Hands in the air now! Move! Move!" barked the agent on the right.

"You can't DO this to US! Didn't you hear him? We are with the CIA!" shouted Curtis, his face reddening to a dangerous shade.

Jorge and Sandy had frozen at the sight of the two Secret Service agents. Without moving, Jorge said, "Gentlemen, I think they can and are doing this. Would you please comply before we all get shot?" Jorge raised his hands above his shoulders. Sandy hesitated then followed suit.

"You are going to hear about this!" Harold sputtered as he reluctantly raised his hands.

With a muttered curse, Curtis did the same.

One agent covered them as the second took their guns, then patted everyone down. Sandy met Jorge's eyes as rough hands pushed and pulled her body. He gave a microscopic head shake no.

With a glance around them, the agents swiped the door lock and opened the suite again.

"Inside. All of you." growled the lean, humorless agent with dark hair.

They crowded through the doorway into an ornate foyer. The door clicked shut behind them.

One agent kept his gun raised and ready as the second muttered into his wrist.

Curtis opened his mouth to speak.

"Silence!" barked the other agent, a muscular sandy-haired man who was also singularly lacking in humor.

Curtis wisely shut up.

There was motion behind them. Buford Wagner stood in the doorway, a scowl on his face.

His eyes raked the little group, pausing briefly on Sandy and Jorge with a look of puzzlement, then back to the agents where his expression turned to irritation.

"Would you care to come in? You were certainly eager enough a few minutes ago."

Sandy's eyes had narrowed, her face was alight. Jorge snuck a peek at her and groaned internally.

With a last worried glance at her, Jorge allowed himself to be ushered into the main room behind the two CIA agents.

Chapter Forty-Seven

They crowded into the main room of the elegant suite, the agents still tensed and ready to act.

The doors to the two bedrooms were closed.

Buford paced across the length of the room, casting a speculative eye on the two indignant CIA agents. Sandy and Jorge sat poised on one couch: the two agents across from them on the other.

"I'm telling you; you boys think you own the town, but you don't!" sputtered Harold. "The shit is going to hit the fan here!"

"The only 'shit' as you so elegantly put it is the amount you two are currently in." Buford retorted. "So how about you fill me in on why you were trying to break into my suite during a major event?"

"We weren't breaking in! We have important federal business here!"

Buford's eyes were cold. "You want to fill me in on what is so important that you are trying to gain 'unauthorized entry' to the suite of the leading candidate for President and while armed to boot? Are you stupid, man?"

Harold flushed. "We weren't looking for you. We were following those old ladies."

Buford stilled. "What old ladies?" he asked in a dangerously calm tone.

"Those four old women who came up here. Don't pretend you don't know about them. They came up here, to your suite."

Sandy and Jorge stopped breathing.

Buford scowled at Harold. "There aren't any old ladies up here. And that does not explain why you were coming up here."

"I told you we were following them. We've been following them since they left that shit hole town in Vermont they live in."

"And why, pray tell, were you following four old ladies from Vermont?" His voice was icy.

Harold fell silent.

Buford strode across the room and put his face in his. "WELL?"

Harold scowled. "Fuck you." was his reply.

Buford flushed. "You, sir just landed yourself in a world of shit." He glanced at Curtis. "As well as your partner. I hope you enjoy being assigned to Jefferson City Missouri for the rest of your career. If you even HAVE a career after this."

"Now wait just a minute!" Curtis blurted, "I'll tell you why we were here! It's because we were following Richard Haverill, that's why! And the last place we tracked him was to their home!"

Sandy and Jorge exchanged a look.

Buford stared at Curtis with a stony expression. "Why were you tracking Haverill?"

"Where is he? Did he show up yet? You can ask him." Curtis said smugly.

Buford stared at him deadpan. "As a matter of fact, he did and I will. But I'd also like to hear what your take on the matter is as well."

Harold looked up his jaw dropping slightly. "Huh? He's here?"

"Yes, he's here. Now what's it going to be, boys? D.C. or Jefferson City?" Buford folded his arms.

Harold looked at Curtis and shrugged. "I guess if he's here it doesn't matter as much now. We thought he had been kidnapped. And we have our orders..." he trailed off and looked at Sandy and Jorge.

Buford turned to look at them too. "I neglected to ask who these two are."

Jorge straightened his shoulders and tipped his chin back. "Sir, I am Don Habero, a doorman at this fine hotel and this," he reached out and touched Sandy's arm, "Is Irena Alamonde, one of our housekeeping staff. These gentlemen," he nodded toward the two agents, "demanded our assistance in the hallway when we were on our way to another room."

Buford looked at Sandy. "So how long have you been working here, Irena?"

Jorge interjected smoothly. "I'm sorry, she doesn't speak English."

"Then your ID's will work just fine." Buford held his hand out.

ID's. ID's neither of them had.

Jorge and Sandy went still.

"I, uh, I don't carry mine when I work, and I don't think Sa...Irena does either. Too many chances to lose it."

Buford's eyes narrowed.

There was a tapping in the hallway. "Housekeeping."

"Jesus." Buford muttered. "Get rid of them." He said to the tall agent.

He holstered his gun and headed to the foyer. They heard a murmuring of voices.

The agent reappeared. "Sir, Mr. Rock wanted that table disinfected."

Buford made an exasperated sound. "Let her in then. But these four go in the other room first." He jerked his head toward the other bedroom.

The short agent trained his gun on them. "No funny business."

They herded them into an opulent bedroom with a canopy bed and fireplace.

As they closed the door behind them, Sandy saw Buford opening the door to the master bedroom.

She saw a splash of hot pink just before the door closed.

Chapter Forty-Eight

The door clicked shut behind them.

Sandy wheeled on the feds, her eyes blazing. "Alright, tell me right now what was going on with Richard Haverill and those four ladies."

"Wait! What? You aren't supposed to speak any English!" Harold sputtered.

"Surprise, surprise!" Sandy glared at them. "Looks like I do. So, tell me, what the hell is going on here?"

Curtis had flushed a dark red. "I don't know who the two of you are, but it doesn't involve you!"

"It most certainly does." Sandy countered. "Those 'old ladies' as they were called are my friends."

"So who the hell are YOU?" Curtis snarled. "And how did you know about the old ladies?"

"Geeze, you keep calling them that and I'll see to it they know about it. Trust me, you don't want those women on your case. So, what the hell happened between them and Richard Haverill?"

Curtis and Harold exchanged looks.

"You two REALLY aren't in a bargaining position here." Sandy said.

"Well neither are YOU!" Harold snapped, glaring at her.

Jorge shifted on the couch uncomfortably. "Gentlemen, we are members of the press. And we are protected by Amendment 1.9.1 which states in part, 'Congress shall make no law respecting an establishment of religion or prohibiting free expression thereof; or abridging the freedom of the press...etcetera, etcetera.' And right now, our freedom of speech is being abridged. Now you two may have careers on the line, but I can assure you, ours aren't. However, if we are detained much longer, the shit is going to hit the proverbial fan. So, what's it going to be, boys? Stonewall us and your only chance of getting out of this intact or telling us why you had surveillance on Richard Haverill?"

The two agents exchanged looks.

"What media outlet are you from?" Curtis asked.

"The Washington Daily News." Jorge's voice was icy.

Sandy glanced at him but held her tongue. The two agents looked at each other again, calculating looks this time.

"Tell me, what if we promised you an exclusive?" Harold said slowly. "In exchange for getting us out of this mess?"

"I'd have to hear it first." Jorge replied. "Make sure it was worth the trouble."

Curtis scowled. "And how do we know we can trust you?"

Sandy looked at Jorge and said, "Because this is Jorge Maxim. You may have heard of him before. You know, the

Pulitzer winner for his expose on events in that same small Vermont town these women are from?"

Harold looked at Jorge with interest. "I heard about that. I read your articles. You did that series on human trafficking last year. I do know about you."

He swung his gaze to Sandy. "I don't know about YOU though."

Jorge waved his hand dismissively. "Sandy Case, new hire at the News. Now tell me what is going on with Haverill? If it's good, my boss will lean on their bosses and get you two out from under."

"And if it isn't good in your eyes?" Harold retorted.

"Then you better make it good, right?" Jorge replied.

Curtis sighed and shrugged. "To hell with it. We're already screwed." He looked at Harold who looked down at his hands. "So, about eight months ago, we got assigned to shadow Haverill. Follow him wherever he went, listen to everything he said."

"Why would they want you to do that?" Sandy asked.

"It's not uncommon." Harold said, "Especially if there are any doubts about someone's efficacy, and I guess they were having doubts about his."

"Doubts about him why?" Jorge asked.

"The powers that be weren't sure they could trust him in a position of power. They were worried about his mouth and his dick, if you catch my drift." Curtis said.

"Seems like a wandering dick is a trademark of all politicians." Sandy interjected.

"Yeah, well, more so in this case. That man's dick took side trips into women all across the country. They were worried he could be compromised by the Russians because of it. And we all know how that goes."

They all fell silent for a moment.

Curtis continued. "We were following him from stop to stop on the tour. Then we hit the last one, the New Hampshire one." Curtis glared at Harold. "By the New Hampshire event, we had already been to eighteen others, so we weren't as on our game as we could have been. Someone just had to stop and get a chili cheese dog, so we did. I had one too, and it messed our guts up. We were at the event but were both in the men's room when Haverill disappeared."

Harold sniffed. "I seem to recall YOU were just as eager for that dog as I was."

Curtis glared at him. "Thanks to you, I will NEVER eat one of those again!"

Harold looked at Jorge and Sandy. "So how do YOU two fit in?"

"I told you, they're our friends. And they would never be involved in anything."

"Well apparently Haverill is back here now." Harold said. "I honestly don't know what to make of that one."

"Me either." Said Sandy.

"I want to know where the women are. We were told they were here." Jorge said.

"Told by who?" Harold asked.

Jorge was shaking his head. "Confidential sources." He said.

"Oh sure," Harold said, "We tell YOU what WE know but you won't tell US what YOU know."

"Sanctity of the press." Jorge replied.

"They're here, right now." Sandy said.

"What?" Curtis's head snapped up, "How do YOU know that?"

Ignoring Jorge's glare, Sandy continued. "Because we saw them outside, and we saw what they were wearing. One of them has on a hot pink dress. When Buford went into the other room, I saw a glimpse of hot pink as he opened the door."

"Son of a bitch." Harold said looking at Curtis. "Did you see Haverill with them?"

Sandy looked at Jorge who simply glowered at her and didn't speak. Narrowing her eyes she replied, "I don't know if it was Haverill, but they were pushing someone in a wheelchair who looked like a man."

"Damn it all." Curtis muttered, just as the bedroom door swung open.

Buford Wagner was standing in it. He glared at the agents. "You two. Get out."

They glanced at each other and leapt to their feet. "You haven't heard the last of this!" Harold snarled.

"Oh, I think we have." Buford replied acidly.

Jorge and Sandy scrambled to their feet. "Hey, what about us?" Jorge said.

Buford was shaking his head. "I still need to find out who you two are."

"Hey!" Jorge called to the retreating backs of the two agents. "Tell them who we are!"

Harold glanced over his shoulder. "I don't know who they are; they're hotel staff." They disappeared.

"Why those rotten..." Jorge sputtered.

Buford gestured to the room he was standing in.

"Get out here."

Sandy looked across the space to the master bedroom.

The door was open, and it was empty.

Chapter Forty-Nine

Sandy and Jorge sat rigidly on the couch as Buford paced the room, a pistol in his right hand.

The Secret Service agents were gone.

He strode across the small space to the bar where he poured himself a shot of whiskey.

He tossed it back in one smooth move.

Sandy fidgeted next to Jorge. He placed a warning hand on her knee.

Buford stalked back across the room, visibly fighting back anger.

"I have had about enough surprises here tonight. I called down to the manager about you two, and guess what he told me? They don't have anyone on the staff who resembles either one of you. So, drop the games. Who are you?"

He swung the gun around and leveled it at them. "You have ten seconds."

Jorge paled and his fingers clenched. A bead of sweat popped out on his temple.

Sandy scowled at Buford. "Oh, for Pete's sake. Drop the he-man routine already."

Jorge gasped next to her.

Buford's fingers tightened on the gun, his finger slipping off the guard and onto the trigger. "I thought you didn't speak English?"

"Surprise, surprise. Looks like I do! Where are the women?"

Buford's face paled as he leveled the gun at Sandy. Jorge drew his breath in sharply.

Sandy raised her chin defiantly. "So, what are you gonna do here, shoot the press?"

"The...press?" Buford's forehead crinkled as the implication of her words hit him. "The press? Who ARE you two?"

Defiantly Sandy replied, "Sandra Case from the Brownville Reporter and Jorge Maxim from the Washington Daily News, that's who."

Buford stared at them for a long moment then swore softly. Slipping the safety on, he shoved the gun into the holster hidden under his coat.

"What the HELL are YOU TWO doing here then?"

"Where are the women?" Sandy's voice was icy.

"What women?"

"Don't give me that. We followed them here, and I saw them in that room." She jerked her head toward the master bedroom. "So, where the hell are they?"

Buford ran a hand over his close-cropped hair and stared at them for a long moment.

Sandy raised her chin and stared back at him steadily.

She noticed a tremor in his left hand as he curled his fingers into a fist and placed them on his hip.

He opened his mouth to speak.

From the hallway came a commotion. Buford jerked at it, reaching under his coat toward his gun. There was motion in the doorway; the sandy-haired Secret Service agent apologetically saying, "I'm sorry sir, but there are police in the hallway, and they are quite insistent that they be allowed entry."

Buford's eyes narrowed.

"Send them in. I have two people trespassing here, anyway. They can deal with them."

The agent returned to the door and muttered something. The door to the hall burst open and Jim rushed into the room with two D.C. officers behind him.

"Sandy! Jorge! Are you two alright?"

Buford scowled. "Who are you?"

Jim drew himself upright and pinned a glare on Buford. "I'm Officer Jim Pim and I am here about those ladies. Now where are they?"

"What is with the obsession with those old women?" Buford rolled his eyes.

"Where are they?" Jim demanded.

"Well, they aren't here and never were despite what your psychopath friends here are saying. Go ahead and search the place if you don't believe me!" He turned away from them, folding his arms and staring out the window.

The dark- haired agent stepped up next to Jim. He jerked his chin toward the suite. With a glance at him, Jim disappeared into the master bedroom.

As he searched, Sandy glared at Buford's back and said, "You better not have harmed so much as a single gray hair on their heads."

Without turning around Buford replied, "I told you. They aren't here and they never were."

Jim emerged from the second bedroom and made eye contact with Sandy. He shook his head no.

"Now will you all please get the hell out of here? I have

a function to attend." Buford said, his back still to them.

Chapter Fifty

Three months later

Doris carefully placed her teacup on the table and settled down into her couch. Rita was ensconced in her favorite armchair, a new knitting project, this one in shades of purple and yellow in her hands.

Doris glanced over at her. "Another afghan?"

Rita nodded as she turned the piece this way and that. "Yes. Betty always liked these colors, and it's getting really cold now. She can use it as a lap robe."

Doris sighed as she picked up the television remote. "I know it's for the best, but I still miss her."

"I for one, miss Frankie." Lily said as she entered the room.

"Oh, my Lord, that...THING!" Doris shuddered.

"Why in the world would you miss THAT?" Rita asked. "I can tell you I DON'T miss the noise all night long!",

Lily smiled, a slow ear to ear grin. "Remember the

Brownville PD the day I chased them out of the house with it? Or when Betty cold cocked that would be thief? Ha!"

"Lily." Doris's voice held a warning note. "Lily, you know we signed that agreement to never speak of any of that."

"But we are in our own home. Who's gonna know?" Lily asked.

Doris was shaking her head firmly. "We simply can't risk it. Our futures...and especially Betty's...depend on our discretion."

"Well, I still say we did 'em a favor." Lily grumbled as she sat down on the couch. "Ricky was one worthless man when he was alive."

On the television, shots of frozen spectators thronging the Washington Monument filled the screen.

"They're saying it's a record turnout for the inauguration." Rita said.

On the screen, Horace Rock and his wife climbed the stairs to the Capitol, resplendent in their finery. On the top of the steps, Ricky Haverill in his ever-present sunglasses was already seated in his wheelchair, his wife clutching his gloved hand. To the ladies, he looked awfully still. To the public, they wouldn't even notice it, nor would they realize his wife always had his hand and that any motion from him came from her subtle movements.

Doris shook her head. "Of all the possible outcomes, I still cannot believe that Horace Rock would be elected with Richard Haverill as his VP." She said.

Lily slouched down in the couch crossing her right ankle on her knee. "I think he's better now than he was when he was al..."

"Lily!" Doris barked. "Stop talking about that!"

"Geeze Louise!" Lily rolled her eyes. "And it's okay if YOU do?"

"Do you think Hiram would appreciate having that fancy new job with the feds getting pulled out from under him like that?" Rita asked.

Lily scowled and fell silent.

Doris huffed and reached for her tea as they held the Bible up to Horace Rock. He placed one hand on it and began reciting an oath.

There was a hard rapping sound at the back door.

"Oh, now what?" sputtered Doris. It sometimes felt like no one ever left them alone anymore.

"I'll get it." Rita said. She rose up and headed through the swinging door into the kitchen.

On the television, cheers rose as Horace finished his oath. A speaker stepped up to the podium as the Rita pushed her way through the swinging doors, her expression pained.

Behind her was Sandy Case.

Lily didn't bother hiding her groan.

"Nice to see you again, Miz Harris." Sandy said acerbically.

She dropped her bag on the floor with a thud and flopped down on the couch next to Lily.

"Why thank you, I'd love some tea." She said.

"You aren't staying that long." Doris said placidly.

Sandy glowered at her. "What happened with Richard Haverill?" she asked, as if she hadn't peppered them with variants of that question for the past three months.

Doris kept her gaze trained on the television. "Why he just became Vice President of the United States is what happened to him." She waved at the screen.

Sandy snorted, an exasperated noise. "You know I'm going to find out, right?"

"There's nothing to find out, dear." Said Rita as she resumed her knitting.

"Nothing to find out? The leading candidate for the Vice Presidency of the United States went missing for a week, was last seen getting into a car with Betty and suddenly, he's back and mysteriously Betty is in Sunshine Acres, the most expensive nursing care home in the state, and there's nothing to find out? Where'd she get the money for that?"

"Oh, I don't know, I guess her ex left her some when he passed a few years ago." Doris said calmly.

Sandy slapped the arm of the couch in frustration. "I KNOW I saw you in Buford's suite that night."

"How could you have possibly seen us, dear? We weren't there." Doris lifted her cup to her lips as a whirring sound from the front staircase echoed through the room.

Lily made a subtle grimace.

"You ladies are up to no good. I know it!" Sandy muttered.

From the hallway came a clunking, thumping noise as Donna Green made her way into the parlor. The light reflected off her high forehead and glasses. She scowled at Sandy.

"You're in my seat, Missy!"

Doris looked at Sandy as she rose and said in a resigned tone, "Sandy, we aren't up to anything. We're just a bunch of old ladies doing our best to make it in this world."

About the Author

Stevie Lynne is the alter ego of writer Stephanie Funk. Stevie and Stephanie make their home in western Massachusetts with her husband Ed and a variety of furry and feathered family members.